REALITY CHECK IN DETROIT

ROY MacGREGOR AND KERRY MacGREGOR

Tundra Books

Text copyright © 2015 by Roy MacGregor and Kerry MacGregor

Published in Canada by Tundra Books, a division of Random House of Canada Limited,
One Toronto Street, Suite 300, Toronto, Ontario M5C 2V6

Published in the United States by Tundra Books of Northern New York,
P.O. Box 1030, Plattsburgh, New York 12901

Library of Congress Control Number: 2014941837

Library and Archives Canada Cataloguing in Publication

MacGregor, Roy, 1948-, author
    Reality check in Detroit / Roy MacGregor.

(Screech Owls)
Issued in print and electronic formats.
ISBN 978-1-77049-422-0 (pbk.).–ISBN 978-1-77049-427-5 (epub)

    I. Title. II. Series: MacGregor, Roy, 1948- . Screech Owls series.

PS8575.G84R42 2015   jC813'.54   C2014-903061-4
                                                   C2014-903062-2

Designed by Jennifer Lum

www.tundrabooks.com
www.penguinrandomhouse.ca

Printed and bound in the United States of America

1 2 3 4 5 6   20 19 18 17 16 15

For Olivier and for Ellen, with appreciation

1

Travis Lindsay's eyes had finally fixed on the perfect postcard – a moody black-and-white photo of a boxer slouched in the corner of a ring, holding two shiny black boxing gloves up in front of his chest – when Wayne Nishikawa poked his head around the postcard rack, slid a pair of bejeweled butterfly sunglasses down his nose, and announced his new life plan.

"From now on, you can call me Hollywood!"

"Um . . . Nish, that's not going to happen," Travis laughed.

Travis picked up the postcard of Joe Louis, the boxer the Detroit Red Wings' hockey rink had been named after, flipped it over, and then put it back.

"You know those are girl glasses, right?"

"*Girl glasses?* Not once I make them famous!" Nish said loudly, shifting his eyes back and forth as if the paparazzi might be after him.

"*Nish?* A teen heartthrob? Um . . . no thanks!" Sarah Cuthbertson called from the line of Screech Owls waiting to pay for their Stupid Stop purchases. She had found a windup flashlight keychain that fitted in the palm of her hand. "You can slow down, egomaniac. The TV crew hasn't even shown any footage of us yet," she added.

"Way before there was Justin Bieber and Michael Jackson, there was Elvis," Nish called back, pushing his sunglasses up his nose again. "Elvis was made fun of . . . and then he was *huge!* – just like that. Just like I'll be!"

Nish shot Sarah his best Elvis-style hip wiggle before holding out his hand to show Travis his

2

other purchase option: a big, ancient-looking tube of hair gel with a dusty orange discount sticker.

"Not that again," Travis groaned, grabbing the tube and slipping it onto a shelf between a dozen Motor City snow globes and mugs. "Your hair gel experiments always smell like egg farts. Go find something else to buy with your money."

"Fine," Nish shrugged.

"Five minutes!" Mr. Dillinger, the Screech Owls' manager, called from the glass doors at the front of the store. "The bus *and* the cameras start rolling again in *five minutes*! If you aren't outside, we're leaving you behind!"

Nish swaggered down one of the narrow souvenir shop aisles and reached out to a rack of skinny black-satin ties and bow ties with "THE TEMPTA-TIONS" written across them in glittery block letters. "I've just gotta have something to set me apart, Trav – you know, other than my good looks and charm. When we get to Detroit – Motown, baby! – you *know* I'm going to have to be the star."

"*Have to?*" Travis chuckled under his breath as he grabbed the Joe Louis postcard for the collection he'd started up after the Owls went to Boston. He also picked out one of a regular-looking, white-and-blue house with the words "HITSVILLE, U.S.A." on it for Muck, the Owls' coach.

Nish, however insufferable, had been working toward his Hollywood goal for the last six weeks, and to Travis's surprise, it seemed to be paying off.

Stardom, or at least a bit of it, seemed finally within reach for Nish.

Back in November, Nish had heard about a reality TV show called *Hit the Ice*. The show featured Aboriginal players from across the country and let them show off their skills, and Nish, seeing an opportunity, had taken Jesse Highboy under his "creative" wing. Jesse, after all, was from James Bay and his family was Cree. And he was a pretty good little hockey player.

As Jesse's "agent," Nish had coaxed Travis and Larry Ulmar – a.k.a. Data – out onto the Lord

Stanley Public School rink to film Jesse's audition tape. Data brought his new camera; Travis was to be the playing partner; Nish would be the director, the agent, and, if he could figure out how to do it, the real star.

First, they did some fancy stickhandling around tiny orange pylons, then a little open-ice, puck-chasing hustle (to show off Jesse's best feature: the fact that he always tried so hard), and then, for good measure, Jesse took shot after shot on a near-empty net – near-empty because Travis was awful in goal. Data had even been able to add in some cool tracking shots by rolling his wheelchair along the outside of the boards while he filmed.

Nish had packaged the audition tape with a quick, comical "between periods interview" with the right-winger, in which Nish got more "face time" than Jesse. Nish then added his own Screech Owls hockey card in place of a business card and dropped the package in the mail.

Two weeks later, they got a reply. The producers didn't just want Jesse Highboy, they wanted *all* of the Screech Owls to appear in their own reality show they planned to call *Goals & Dreams*. And it wouldn't be on the small Aboriginal network in Canada. It would air on national networks all over North America – and the producers had plans to sell the show to Europe and the rest of the world.

For the first time anyone could remember, one of Nish's mad-crazy schemes was actually working out.

He might even end up a true star.

2

Muck, not surprisingly, hadn't been big on the idea of his team being part of a reality television series, but he'd let the parents put it to a vote. Since the Screech Owls had only a four-day skills competition in Detroit between Christmas and New Year's Eve, and because the show had promised to put the players up and feed them, it was hard for any of the parents to say no – even the ones who were a bit unsure about being in the spotlight as part of the players' "lives back home."

What won Muck over were the skills sessions the show had promised. The producers said they would bring together several of the most forward-thinking hockey coaches in the world – one from Sweden, one from Russia, and college coaches from the United States and Canada – to devise a skills competition the likes of which had never been seen on a hockey rink.

There was also the not-so-insignificant matter that Muck, the history buff, would also get to take a closer look at the origins of Detroit's famous Motown recording industry. The great music made in Detroit had been a big part of his youth.

So, in the end, he relented, and to great cheering in the Owls' dressing room back in little Tamarack, he had given the go-ahead with a curt nod of his chin.

The Screech Owls were headed for Detroit . . . and the world of lights, cameras, and action!

"Got it!" Nish said, having snapped one of the black-satin bow ties around his neck. He slid his glittery sunglasses back down his nose. "I look Motown famous, right? *Elvis* famous?"

"You look ridiculous," said Travis, shaking his head at the bow tie and laughing. "Not one of those people ever wore a bow tie over a T-shirt that said, 'PULL MY FINGER.'"

Nish looked down at his shirt – the words over a picture of a giant blue-and-white Toronto Maple Leafs foam finger – and smiled.

"We're *on*!" yelled Mr. D. "*Everyone! Bus! NOW!*"

Travis and Nish finished paying for their Stupid Stop treasures – "Only one rule," Mr. D always told them as he handed them a little pocket money. "You have to buy something absolutely unnecessary and useless" – and together climbed onto the team's old renovated school bus. They were expecting to see a *Goals & Dreams* camera-man with his tripod in the aisle of the bus again, ready to film more of the segment they called "The Screech Owls: Life on the Road." Instead, he was standing next to the driver's seat, holding a TV remote.

"I can't believe it!" Sarah said as Nish straightened his ludicrous bow tie and gave the cameraman his best crooner's smile.

"I don't even know the Klingon phrase for this one," Data sighed. "Maybe '*nuqDaq 'oH puchpa''e?*'"

"What's *that* mean?" asked Fahd Noorizadeh.

"Where's the toilet," Data said, giggling. "Because *I think I'm gonna hurl!*"

"The tie's not *that* bad —" Nish started, more offended that Data had stolen his famous line, but then he realized his teammates weren't even looking at his bow tie. They were staring above it, at one of the bus's small TV screens. On the screen, Nish the hockey superstar, soon to be Hollywood icon, was beaming back at them, in full Screech Owls uniform, from a photo on his mother's piano.

Roger, the cameraman — a short little fellow with curling white hair and a likable smile — was using Mr. D's homemade TV system to show them some raw footage of what the producers had assembled so far in the series.

"*Turn it up!*" Nish shouted. He bowled past Travis to get farther onto the bus, his bow tie bouncing enthusiastically just below his chin.

"He's always been very musical – from piano, to violin . . . ," Mrs. Nishikawa was saying as the camera cut to a shot of Nish adjusting his shin pads in the Screech Owls' dressing room. In the background, Travis and Andy Higgins were re-taping their blades. Wilson Kelly was going over a defense drill with Muck.

"Winning is all about finesse," Nish was saying directly to the camera. "And I'm a finesse player, a finesse defenseman – there aren't many of us. I come out, I play my best, and my best just happens to be really, really awesome. Right now, I'm working on my version of the shootout spin-o-rama – very controversial . . ."

On the bus, Travis and Sarah turned and stared at each other in horror. Data rolled his eyes and groaned loudly.

Nish paid no attention. "Ha!" he shouted over the sound track on the TV. "Do you see that? I'm going to be huge. *Huge!*"

Neither Travis nor Sarah said a word. They just stared at each other, their thoughts perfectly in tune.

They were witnessing the birth of a monster.

A monster called Wayne Nishikawa.

The whole trip had seemed improbable right from the start. Muck agreed to it only because there would be no cost to the team and they'd be promoting skills development. Muck believed in practice, much to Nish's regret. He believed that the two most important elements of good hockey were skill and speed. Muck said minor hockey teams in Canada played far too many games and tournaments and held far too few practices. He liked the European model of hockey, where players practiced two or three times more than they played. Creativity is a simple process, Muck liked to say. You repeat, repeat, repeat, and repeat again — and when it works, people will think you made it up on the spot.

Mr. D was all for the trip. He liked nothing better than to take the old bus out on a road trip and include one of his treasured Stupid Stops. The parents were in favor, too, because it wasn't going to cost them anything. And Nish, of course, was in, because, well, *Goals & Dreams* would help jump-start his Hollywood career.

Travis had dozed off before they reached Windsor, on the Canadian side of the Detroit River. Mr. D woke him up when they came to the border crossing and the Owls' manager had to produce the team's passports. As usual, Lars Johanssen, who carried a Swedish passport, was asked a few questions, but soon enough they were all cleared to go and Mr. D directed the bus down into the brightly lit tunnel that took them under the river to the American side.

Travis rested his head against the window as the yellow lights along the tunnel wall flashed by. He felt like he was in a spaceship, and he might just as well have been – he was about to enter a world so distant from the one he had left it could have been light years away.

Before they went to the hotel to check in, Mr. D gave them a quick tour of the downtown. Travis knew this would have been Muck's suggestion. He had noticed Muck moving to the front of the bus and leaning down to whisper something to Mr. D.

No trip, Muck always said, should ever be just about hockey. You should learn something, too. Something of value. And there was certainly something to learn in their brief look at downtown Detroit. Travis had once seen a movie, *War of the Worlds*, in which it appeared that all humanity had been destroyed. Streets were empty, cars abandoned, storefronts shattered or closed down. It wasn't that bad in downtown Detroit, but it sure wasn't good. Hardly anyone was in the streets, few vehicles were parked, and even fewer were going anywhere. Store after store had "FOR RENT" or "FOR LEASE" signs, or were simply shuttered up with plywood that had faded in the weather.

When they turned onto a particularly bleak

street, Muck indicated to Mr. D that he should pull over and park. He stood up in the middle of the aisle and asked Roger not to record him. He then turned and faced the Owls.

"I want you all to remember what you are seeing here," he said. His voice was quiet, but every single word was heard and understood by the players. "Detroit is what they call a ghost city. When the bottom fell out of the North American automobile industry, the bottom fell out of this city. Today, Detroit has less than half the population it had as far back as 1950. It has a hundred thousand abandoned buildings and houses. It has the highest unemployment and poverty rates of any large city in the United States."

He paused while the Owls took all that in.

"I wanted you to see this," he said, "because I want you to think hard about something . . ." He paused again.

Fahd, of course, asked the obvious. "What?"

Muck looked over all the Owls. None of them dared even to breathe.

"To think about how lucky you are."

3

"*S* *WAG! We got swag! Swag! Swag! Swag! Swag!*" Nish had screamed at the top of his voice, his face a swollen tomato about to burst.

Travis had never thought he might one day say he felt like he had died and gone to . . . Detroit. But this, he had to admit, was Hockey Heaven. Or as close to it as any Screech Owl had ever come.

They had just checked in to a hotel fancier and more luxurious than anything they had ever experienced. The Marriott Renaissance – "Five stars, 72 floors, 1,298 rooms," Data had read from his phone as Mr. Dillinger pulled the bus up in front of the blackest, tallest building on the Detroit waterfront.

At the reception desk in the marble-floored lobby, room keys had already been laid out waiting for the Owls to check in, along with a card telling who would be rooming with whom. *Two to a room!* Travis had never imagined such luxury – usually the Owls were four to a room, sometimes six. Travis's only possible cause for complaint came when he found his card and key. On the card was written, in flowery script: "ROOM 4715: TRAVIS LINDSAY AND WAYNE NISHIKAWA."

Just his luck, Travis had thought, to draw the stinkiest, loudest, dumbest, craziest, silliest, quirkiest, most troublesome, bothersome, and irritating Owl of them all: his sometimes-best-friend-some-times-worst-enemy, Nish.

Travis forgot his bad luck, however, the moment he slid the key into the lock and their door swung open on a large bright room with two queen-size beds. Each bed had brand-new hockey gear laid out on it.

Nish tossed his suitcase and raced to the nearest bed, then flew through the air as if he were diving into a pool. He screamed as he hit the bed – "*SWAG!*" – and began rolling around with as much hockey equipment as he could hold in his arms.

"Wrong bed," Travis said.

Nish stopped rolling and blinked, not following. "Whaddya mean, wrong bed? You 'n' me's roomies, pal."

"Wrong bed," Travis repeated. He went to the other bed and pulled a hockey jacket off the end and held it up. He had never seen such a beautiful jacket. It was baby blue with black leather arms and it had the Screech Owls' beloved logo over the heart. On the left arm was "PEEWEE AA" and on the right arm was "NO. 44" – and right below that, "NISH."

"*They know me!*" Nish shouted, leaping from Travis's bed to his own and rolling about with the jacket in his arms as if he had just given birth to it.

The "swag" – as Nish called it – was unbelievable. The television producers were providing brand-new equipment to every player on the team. And not just new equipment, but the *best* new equipment.

Travis picked up his own jacket – "NO. 7, TRAVIS" – and tried it on. It fitted perfectly. Nish had put his on, too, and it also fitted perfectly. How could they know our sizes? Travis wondered. They must have gone through Mr. D – Mr. D knew everyone's size, their sticks, and even how they liked their skates sharpened.

Travis checked his stick: a Bauer Vapor, just like he'd dreamed of having one day, but it had been too expensive to ask for. The stick was exactly the lie and curve he liked. He went over the rest of the equipment: top-of-the-line Bauer shoulder pads, shin pads, elbow pads, socks, jock, helmet, face shield, neck guard, pants – even new skates exactly the right size. As well as the team jacket, there was also a Screech Owls tuque, a tracksuit with his name and number on it, and a new NHL-quality Screech Owls jersey. It even had the captain's *C* stitched over the heart.

Nish was still rolling around on his bed in all the new equipment. At one point, he even squealed, which Travis thought appropriate: his friend looked like a happy pig in a trough.

There was a knock at the door.

When Travis pulled it open, he was almost run over by a cameraman and soundman, who both hurried to the bed where Nish was *bathing* in his new hockey swag. Nish, of course, ramped up his foolishness, wiggling as he tried to drown in the equipment, screeching as he hugged and kissed his new gloves and the new black Bauer helmet with "44" stenciled in bright white stick-on numbers on the back.

A familiar voice sounded from the doorway. *"These young hockey hopefuls could one day become legends, heroes of the NHL!"*

Squeezed into the door frame were Samantha Bennett and Sarah, both of them outfitted head to toe in the new equipment. They waltzed in, giggling and laughing, and high-fived Nish, who was still flopping around on his bed as if he had fallen into one of his beloved Dairy Queen Blizzards.

The girls were repeating a line from the *Goals & Dreams* video that the cameraman had played on the bus, the "Voice of God" announcer making it sound like these peewee hockey players were but a slap shot from NHL superstardom.

"*The Screech Owls may hail from the small Canadian town of Tamarack,*" Sam continued, hamming it up for the camera, which was almost in her face, "*but their dreams live here!*"

Daniel, the soundman, who had hung the microphone right over her head to capture every word, now dropped it to his waist. Almost anything the players said could make it onto the show – just not any comments that made fun of it.

"Stop copying our voice-over," snapped Inez, one of the producers, who had appeared in the hallway behind Sarah and Sam. "Roger never should have shown you that rough cut. Say something real. This is reality TV. Tell us how you *feel.*"

Travis knew Sam and Sarah well enough to know when they were just poking fun at themselves and Nish. He could also tell that Inez, who wore a smart-looking dress and high heels, and was impatiently tapping her fingernails on a clipboard, had no sense of humor at all.

"What do you think of all this great stuff?" Inez prompted as she put her phone to her ear to take a call and moved farther down the hall.

"There's . . . there's a lot of . . . stuff here," said Travis, trying to offer something more than mockery to the camera. "It's pretty incredible."

"You know who's incredible?" said Nish, still digging through his loot. "Me. And I deserve all of this gear! Star power, baby."

"Well, that's definitely the kind of reality-TV gold Inez is looking for," laughed Daniel as he swung the microphone back in Nish's direction – where Nish thought it should have been all along.

Nish put his shades on, lay back on all his stuff like he was lounging poolside, and started purring. "What can I do? A star has got to shine," he said.

"Get used to all your gear now, because you'll be using it tomorrow. First call is at 7:00 a.m. sharp," Inez barked as she poked her head back into the room, her phone still attached to her ear.

All of the Owls nodded, except for Nish, who was now wearing his helmet and was busy trying to slide his jock over his jeans.

"Oh, and be on time, because we have a twelve-hour day ahead of us," Inez said, tucking the clipboard under her arm. "And you," she motioned to Nish, "bring the shades."

Travis wasn't sure he liked hearing Inez encourage Nish. It was something the Owls had learned the hard way. When Nish started getting crazy, it was best to ignore him. Whatever you did, you never encouraged Nish.

4

Normally, Travis would have been first on the ice at the Joe Louis Arena. He liked nothing better than to step out onto a clean sheet. He loved to roar down the rink alone and take that first corner, digging in hard and flicking his skates at the end of each stride so that his blades sizzled and, with a bit of luck, tossed up a spray of ice or sometimes even water that had yet to freeze if the Zamboni had just finished.

He wouldn't be first today, though: his

roommate had spent too much time on his hair and fawning over his new equipment. Nish had even taken the time to draw a crooked star on some hotel stationery, write "44" in the middle of it, and stick it on the bathroom door, claiming the room as his own. He had made them late for the short walk along the waterfront to the players' entrance at the back of the arena. When they arrived with Mr. D and two other stragglers, Gordie Griffith and Lars Johanssen, Muck and the others were already there.

They had given their names to the security guard and then walked along the corridor to where Muck and the other Owls were gathered. All the Owls had their new tracksuits and jackets on and were carrying their bags of new equipment and their sticks. Muck stood out like a sore thumb: same old hockey windbreaker, same baggy pants. He had, however, put on a clean shirt.

Mr. D had a fancy new jacket that had "MR. D" and "MGR" on the sleeve. Travis knew that somewhere there would be a large, brand-new hockey jacket with "MUCK" and "COACH" on the arm. Likely hanging in Muck's closet back at the hotel. Maybe stuffed in a corner, out of sight. Travis wasn't surprised: the one thing the Owls could absolutely depend on was that Muck would never change.

"I want you to follow me," Muck was telling the Owls, "and use your eyes, not your mouths."

He stared hard, once, in Nish's direction and led the Owls down the twisting corridor until they came to a brightly lit area entirely painted in red and white, the colors of the Detroit Red Wings. He stopped in front of a wall with "HOCKEYTOWN" written on it in large red letters. "HOME OF THE 1997, 1998, 2002 & 2008 STANLEY CUP CHAMPIONS."

"Wow!" exclaimed Fahd. "Four Stanley Cups."

"Eleven," Muck corrected him. "The Joe replaced the Olympia, the old rink where Gordie Howe and Ted Lindsay won cups. The Red Wings have won eleven times."

"Wow again!" said Fahd.

Travis said nothing. But inside he was glowing. Muck had just mentioned Terrible Ted Lindsay, Travis's distant relative. Gordie Howe's line mate. Stanley Cup champion. There were even statues of both Gordie Howe and Ted Lindsay in the Joe.

"Read the names," Muck told them, pointing to the list of players that had been on each of the Cups. "The only way I know for a hockey player to live forever is to have your name on this Cup."

Nish walked up so close to one of the lists that his nose was almost touching it. He seemed to be squinting, reading furiously.

"You won't find 'Nishikawa' there!" Sam laughed.

"It'll be there one day," Nish snapped back.

"Only if you change your name to Stanley," Sarah giggled.

Nish gave both girls the full raspberry.

"Let's get ready," Muck told them. "We're on the ice in fifteen."

"Hollywood has . . . arrived!"

Nish slammed open the door of the Screech Owls' dressing room and stepped out onto the rubber carpeting of the Joe, preening as though he were stepping onto the red carpet at the Oscars. The only thing missing was the wild clicking and whirring of the paparazzi's cameras as they shot photographs of the twelve-year-old celebrity's arrival, and a beautiful blonde in an evening gown gushing all over him as she interviewed him.

Nish ambled along the corridor and down the chute toward the ice surface, mindful to stick to the rubber mat for fear of wrecking Mr. D's careful skate sharpening on the concrete. He held his new black Bauer helmet out like a trophy with one hand and ran his other hand along the side of his head, smoothing out his Elvis-style pompadour.

Nish was dressed for superstardom.

The Screech Owls had played the Motors once before in a tournament. The Motors had been quick and well coached and a good test for the Owls, but that tournament had been the previous season, and teams could sometimes change considerably in a year. The Owls had no idea what to expect this time

"What are you going to do with your bow tie while you play?" asked Travis, stepping out of the chute with Nish and approaching the gate. "Wear it on your butt like a lucky rabbit tail?"

"Ha-ha," Nish responded with a gentle elbow

to Travis's gut. He lifted his throat protector to reveal that he was still wearing the bow tie around his neck. And when he pushed a button on the side of the sparkly black tie, it lit up like a winning slot machine.

"This superstition stuff is serious," Nish said to Travis as they prepared to step out onto the shiny ice of the Joe. "I even flushed the blade of my stick – my *new* stick – for a little extra luck."

The flashing lights on his bow tie stopped and he tucked it back under his throat protector.

"I'm going to nail my spin-o-rama during this skills comp," he said. "I have to. The television audience will love it!"

Travis was sick of hearing about Nish's spin-o-rama move. Ever since the Owls had seen some NHLer use it during a shootout on TV, he'd been trying it in practice, sometimes falling flat on his butt, sometimes losing the puck as he suddenly reversed direction and tried to loop the puck around on his backhand. Once, he'd completed it perfectly but was in so tight to the net that Jenny Staples had just stood there giggling as Nish realized he had no place to shoot. Jenny simply fell to her knees, her big goal pads smothering the puck.

Still, Nish was determined to master it.

Travis shook his head as he did a little skip out onto the ice, turning quickly and skating backward away from Nish and his starry-eyed schemes.

"Don't keep them waiting, Hollywood!"

5

Still skating backward so he could see how Nish tackled his awkward combination of sunglasses and helmet, Travis listened for the delicious sound of pucks slapping on fresh ice. He knew without even turning that Mr. D would be tossing pucks over the boards for the warm-up. Travis turned fast and hard and skated to the growing bunch of pucks, kicked one up onto his stick blade, swooped in, and rang a wrist shot off the crossbar.

First shot and he heard a *clang* of the metal – it was going to be a good day for Travis Lindsay. He felt great. He loved his new equipment. His new skates were so light it felt like they weren't even there – almost as if a steel blade had grown from the bottom of his bare foot. Nish had told Travis his new skates were so comfortable he wasn't even wearing socks, something he claimed the legendary Bobby Orr had done when he played a million years ago.

Nish finally abandoned his sunglasses on the Owls' bench in favor of his shiny Bauer helmet. He seemed to be loving his new equipment, too. With an Elvis-style wiggle of his hips – to the cameras, of course – he scooped up one of Mr. D's pucks and took several hard strides before trying his beloved spin-o-rama move. First try, he lost the puck. Second try, he lost his footing and fell flat on his face.

With Jeremy Weathers and Jenny taking shots from the other Owls, Nish moved his spin-o-rama practice to center ice, where he fell again and committed one of hockey's greatest sins: he slid across the center line into the Detroit Motors' warm-up territory, where an assistant coach was setting up pylons for a stickhandling drill.

Nish took out several of the pylons.

"Hey, Clumsy – get your big butt outta here!" the young coach shouted.

Nish got up sheepishly and skated back to his own side of center. "Agh! Don't worry about me . . . ," the coach shouted. "I'll just set it all up *again*."

Travis noticed that the Detroit player who came over to help gather the scattered pylons was even taller than the coach. The kid must have been nearly six feet tall. Travis took note of the name and number on the somewhat worn-looking Motors jersey: NO. 22, KELLY.

Usually, when Travis looked across the ice at another peewee team, he'd see a bunch of kids roughly the same size as the Owls. Maybe one or two would be taller, maybe a couple smaller than the rest. Nish, of course, was wider than any of the other Owls. But the Motors had four *giants* in their lineup. Really big players who towered over the others.

On top of that, number 22 seemed to be extremely talented: once the pylons were in place again, the tall player crisscrossed his way down the pylon line with a speed and fluidity Travis had never before witnessed. This guy skated like an artist. Sarah and Sam watched with their mouths wide open, and even Nish took a moment to marvel at the player's skill.

Then, at the final pylon, number 22 did something Travis had always dreamed of doing – something he'd never even seen another hockey player do. He turned his feet out so his left skate faced directly left and his right skate faced directly right, and he curled around the pylon like a sharp knife peeling an apple.

"*Whoa!*" shouted Sam, and she and Sarah hammered their sticks on the ice in appreciation. Number 22 looked over and saluted with a big smile and a raised stick.

Nish, of course, couldn't stand it when people paid attention to someone else. Having recovered from his wipeout, he picked up the puck again, raced back close to center ice, launched his spin-o-rama move, and, very slowly . . . pulled it off! He'd spun in a complete circle and still had the puck on his stick. He hadn't scored, but he hadn't fallen. He skated over to the boards, banging his stick on the ice in admiration of his own move.

"Nish is very religious, you know," Sarah said to Sam and Travis.

"I don't think so," Travis said, not following.

"Well, he obviously worships himself."

"A church with a congregation of one," Sam added with a giggle.

Travis giggled, too, but he was watching the other team rather than Nish's desperate bid for attention. The more he thought about it, the more he realized that number 22's height and skill level weren't all that seemed odd. The Motors, unlike the Owls, didn't have brand-spanking-new Bauer equipment. Some of them even wore socks that didn't match: one girl had on blue Maple Leafs socks; a couple were in red Detroit Red Wings socks; and one player was in the red, white, and blue of the Montreal Canadiens.

If this had been a real game, Travis would have wondered what was going on. All the teams the Owls played had matching colors.

"There's kind of a funny vibe here, don't you think?" Sarah whispered to Travis once number 22 had moved on to stickhandling, at which he wasn't at all impressive, losing the puck almost constantly as he tried to work it back and forth. Travis was leaning against the boards, stretching his hamstrings now that his muscles were a little warm. "There's something weird about the way the Detroit Motors are moving around the ice. I can't figure it out."

Travis shrugged and tried to look casual, not like they were gossiping about the other team.

"And what's with their equipment? I mean, why isn't it new, like ours?" asked Sarah, quietly trying to maintain his attention.

Travis gave Sarah a look. She had noticed it, too. "Muck said that Detroit is poor," he said. "That the whole city's suffering and that we should count ourselves lucky."

"Yeah, but why are we luckier than they are?"

Sarah said, tugging at her new jersey, the NHL-quality Bauer jersey in the Screech Owls' red and black colors, the crest on it thick and solid. The jersey even had the loose ties at the neck, just like the NHLers had. "This swag just came with the show – didn't they get any?"

Again, Travis shrugged.

Another one of the big Detroit Motors' players took a shot. It pinged so loudly off the crossbar it made Fahd jump. Travis was impressed. He could never fire a puck like that. The player – number 98, Smith – started doing tricks from center ice. He got down on his knees and began lobbing pucks so high that, after numerous attempts, one landed, and stuck, on the top of the net. Travis had heard that a Russian player, Alexei Kovalev, who had once played for Ottawa, could do that regularly, but he'd never seen anything like it in a peewee practice.

Compared to the Detroit Motors, the Owls' warm-up was barely a spark. Muck had put a stick across two pylons, and the players skated up, hopped over it while the puck slid underneath, and then they had to keep it going. He had them practice skating in patterns around the circles, the drill that always made Travis think of a formation of swallows in flight. And they practiced their passes. But none of that was as fancy as what the other players were doing.

Weren't there supposed to be some inspirational European or Russian coaches on *Goals & Dreams*? Travis remembered Muck being interested in that. But if they were here, shouldn't they be out on the ice? Travis looked over at Muck and noticed that the muscle on the side of Muck's cheek was flexing in and out. His jaw only flexed like that when he was working hard not to say anything.

Travis and Sarah skated over to where the other Owls were taking shots on Jenny just as Mr. D called them over to the Owls' bench. They all crowded around.

Inez, the producer who had come up to their hotel rooms with her clipboard, was standing beside Mr. D. She looked so out of place at a hockey rink that Travis had to tell himself not to giggle. She had on three different necklaces and was wearing rings so large she couldn't have pulled on hockey gloves. She looked as if she were dressed for dinner at an expensive restaurant, not a cold and drafty hockey rink. Travis could see there were goose bumps all the way down her neck. Her neck seemed strained, as if she were yelling but not yelling.

"Inez wants a word with you all," Mr. D said, turning to the woman as his mustache bounced into a welcoming smile. "Inez?"

"Thank you," Inez began. "I wanted to explain something important to all you children."

Children? Travis winced. The Screech Owls weren't babies.

"You may have noticed that the other side doesn't entirely match," she said. "It's really quite unfortunate, but the supplier didn't come through as they did for you. Their new equipment is on back order and we're hoping it will still get here in time. I would appreciate it if you didn't say anything about it – about the fact that you got all this great stuff for free. We want to be able to capture their surprise on camera, when their new equipment gets here, understand? So can I have your word that you won't bring it up? Promise?"

"We promise," said Fahd.

Several of the other Owls muttered their agreement.

"Fine," said Inez. "I appreciate that. Not a word, then, okay?"

"Okay," Fahd said.

Inez turned and began to walk away, likely heading for a warm production room. Travis shook his head and looked at Sarah, expecting her to say something about the way Inez had been dressed.

But Sarah wasn't thinking about any such thing.

"Why is it I don't believe a word that comes out of that woman's mouth?" Sarah said to him.

"Oh, and one more thing. . . . Wayne?" Inez said, hurrying back as if she'd forgotten something. She had a fake, pained-looking smile on her face. She walked right up to where Nish was standing in front of the bench, about to step back onto the ice. "We love the chatter. Your one-liners are great. Keep it up. We hear you're calling yourself Hollywood. True?"

"That's right," said Nish, puffed up with pride like a bird during mating season. "It's got star quality."

"Yes, well, we like it, but it's just not the right name for you," Inez purred, trying to sound like she was giving Nish a compliment. "For the purposes of the show – for the dramatic arc of *Goals & Dreams* – we're going to give that name to Cody Kelly, number 22 on the Detroit Motors. I'm sure you understand. You we'll call . . . Money."

6

Travis had never seen Nish on such a roll. The Owls were walking around the concourse of the Joe, waiting for the first round of competition. Several of them were looking for the statues of Gordie Howe and Ted Lindsay – Travis wanted a photo of himself with Terrible Ted – and Nish was well into a nonstop monologue about himself.

"Love it!" Nish was saying. "*Money* is the perfect nickname for me. I've been a 'money player' since my first season, you guys all know that. If Muck needs to turn a game around, who does he turn to? Me, of course! The old Nisherama is who! Money! You get into overtime, who do you want on the ice? Money, that's who. You go to a shoot-out, who's Muck gonna call on to settle the game? 'Money' Nishikawa! Me! The master of the spin-o-rama. The one guaranteed NHL-bound superstar, hero to millions of little hockey players – me!"

"Oh, put a cork in it," Sam hissed. She'd had enough of the World's Biggest Ego.

"Why is it always about you?" Sarah asked.

"Me?" Nish answered, faking puzzlement while at the same time starting to blush.

"You! It's always about you. You! You! *You!*"

Nish shrugged. He looked genuinely con-fused. "Well, you wouldn't want it to be about Trav, would you? I mean, how boring would that be? Sorry, Trav."

Travis just shook his head and continued on in search of the statues. Up ahead, he could see Gordie Howe's bronzed head. Terrible Ted would be right beside Gordie.

But there was someone else there. The tall kid from the Motors was taking photos with his phone. He was with another player, a smaller kid, but tough-looking, dark, and brooding. He scowled when he noticed the Owls coming. But the big kid smiled when he saw Sarah and Sam.

"Hi!" he said. He had curly blond hair, an open smile, and, it seemed to Travis, an accent. He couldn't quite place it.

The tall player's teammate didn't smile. He didn't say a word. He pretended he was busy taking a selfie with the statue of Gordie Howe.

Data pulled out his smartphone like the rest of the players and snapped a photo of Gordie's head, then started typing a message to put with the photo. As part of the "reality" experience, Inez had asked both teams to tweet about their experiences in the competition so the other peewee teams watching as the show segments aired each night could follow along. Data, the Owls' resident technology expert, had taken on the task – even though he'd confided in Travis that he didn't think he'd have much to say.

"Hey, what did you type?" asked the big kid, smiling – any hint of an accent now gone.

"Where did you learn that skating move?" Sarah jumped in, trying to give Data some time to finish typing his update.

The big player's eyebrows rose in question. "What move?"

"The heel-to-heel move when you circled that final pylon," Sam said.

The player nodded. "My parents used to own one of the large malls here. It's pretty much shut down now. It's a great place for in-line skating. That's where I learned it. It's an in-line skating move. We don't live so close to the mall anymore. We had to move to an apartment when the business started failing. But I still go there a lot on my bike. We do tricks. It's cool."

"In-line skating? Looked a lot like figure skating to me. Maybe you could teach Money here how to land a quad," Sarah said.

The big player looked at Nish. "Money" Nishikawa was turning the color of the Joe's bright red walls. "I saw him try one. He just needs a little more practice."

"It's not some fancy-dance figure-skating move," Nish spat in protest. "It's the spin-o-rama – my shootout move."

"It's not your *move*, Big Boy, till you actually do it in a game," said Sam, drawing a quick raspberry from Nish.

"My name's Cody Kelly," the player said, sticking out his hand to shake Sarah's and then the other players' hands.

"I thought it was Hollywood," said Sam.

Cody shook his head. "Yeah, right – not my idea, believe me. They want us all to go by nicknames like we're some NHL team or something."

"I'm Money," Nish announced. "I'm our top player."

Cody's quiet teammate looked at Nish, bewildered. Cody ignored Nish and kept talking. "This here is Jerome Smith – Smitty – and he's probably *our* best player."

Smitty nodded at the Owls but didn't move to shake hands. Smitty was as dark as Cody was golden. He made Travis feel like the Owls had no business being around the statues because Smitty and Cody had been there first.

"Hi," Sarah said, deliberately walking over with her hand out. Sam followed.

Smitty shook their hands and nodded hello. "You got sick equipment," he said.

Data looked up for a second, nervous that the Owls were going to find themselves in an awkward situation, but then went back to snapping photos and typing.

"Yeah," echoed Cody. "All Bauer. All top shelf, man. Sweet."

Sam seemed about to say something, but Sarah lightly pinched her arm. They had to remember the promise they had made to Inez. They weren't to say anything about the swag, because then there would be no surprise when the Motors finally got theirs.

To divert their attention, Travis began getting his smartphone ready to take the photos he wanted. He'd get one with Terrible Ted and send it to his dad, who always claimed Ted Lindsay was a cousin of Travis's grandfather.

"Do you mind, Sarah?" Travis said as he handed her the phone and began moving to the side of the Ted Lindsay statue.

"Well, see you around," said Cody, backing off with his hands in his jacket pockets and offering a parting smile, just for Sarah. Smitty was already walking away.

"Yeah, sure," said Sarah. "Good luck in the competition!"

"You, too," Cody called back before following Smitty down the concourse.

Sarah began fiddling with the camera.

Sam was giggling. "You're blushing!" she shrieked.

"Am not!" Sarah said, hiding her face behind Travis's smartphone.

"Are too!"

Sarah concentrated as hard as she could on capturing the perfect photograph of Travis with his great idol. But she knew her cheeks were bright pink.

7

"I thought the idea was to develop our skills," Muck muttered.

"Maybe if we put the bus in a ditch, Nishikawa can haul us out," Mr. D said, trying to make light of the matter. But all the same, Mr. Dillinger always knew when Muck was not amused.

The two men were going over a flip chart detailing the various skill competitions the teams would be taking part in this afternoon. The producers had left a movable blackboard in the Owls' dressing room at the Joe, with a description of each skill competition written on it and the names of the players who would compete. Each contest was a segment of *Goals & Dreams: Part One*.

Travis sat beside Sarah at their lockers – complete with each player's name and number tagged at the top, just like in the NHL – and together they read through the list.

> *Speed Challenge*: Once around the rink, carrying puck. Must navigate slalom of pylons in neutral zone. Screech Owls competitors: Sarah Cuthbertson, Travis Lindsay, Dmitri Yakushev.

"Our whole line," Sarah said, smiling. Travis smiled, too. He wasn't nearly as fast as either Sarah or Dmitri, but he knew they were considered a fast hockey line, and he was proud to be included.

They read on:

> *Skating Agility*: A difficult course. Competitors must show agility and inven-

tiveness. Screech Owls competitor: Lars Johanssen.

Hardest Shot: Shots to be measured by major-league baseball radar gun. Screech Owls competitor: Andy Higgins.

Target Shoot: Hit all four Styrofoam targets in corners of net. Maximum number of shots from slot allowed: Ten. Minimum number of shots wins. Screech Owls competitors: Samantha Bennett, Jesse Highboy.

Search and Rescue: Players to be blindfolded while teammates guide to destination by calls. Screech Owls competitor: Fahd Noorizadeh.

Goalie Race: Goaltenders race in full equipment, hitting allowed. Screech Owls competitors: Jenny Staples, Jeremy Weathers.

Tractor Pull: Strength competition. Player must tow teammates on a platform. Winner to be decided on how much he/she can tow. Screech Owls competitor: Wayne Nishikawa.

"I don't know what it is, but it isn't hockey," Muck grunted. He walked away, closing the door to the dressing room as he left. Mr. D went back to his portable skate-sharpening machine and began whistling while he worked on the players' new skates.

"Love it!" Nish shouted, once he was sure Muck was out of earshot. "I get the final event – the climax of the whole skills competition. Me, Money, all alone. It'll be like my guitar solo – give me a little time to show off!"

"As a tractor?" Sam said.

"The only thing *tractor* about you, Money Boy," said Sarah, "is you both give off bad fumes."

Nish shot a raspberry at her and went off to the washroom, almost hugging himself as he walked.

"Only some of the skills are hockey," Fahd said.

"Yeah," said Andy, "but don't forget it's a TV show. It's really about entertainment."

"Some of the competitions sound like fun," Data added. "I just wish I could play."

No one said anything. There was nothing anyone could say.

The ice was freshly flooded when the Owls went back out for the first round of the competition. Roger, the cameraman, the older man with curly white hair, who said he used to work on *Hockey Night in Canada*, stayed with the Owls, shooting everything: Travis getting dressed in his ritual way – right, left, right, left – pulling on his new Owls jersey with the *C* on it; the various shin-tapping rituals all the skaters went through with the two goalies. And then they all filed out onto the ice following Jeremy and Jenny.

Roger came right out onto the ice with Travis. He held his camera down low to catch Travis's stride as the Screech Owls' captain dug in and flew down the ice, turning hard into the corner. Travis looked up into the stands, surprised to see fans taking their seats for the competition. They must be family and friends of the Motors. None of the

Owls' parents had come, knowing they'd get to experience the trip on television as the episodes aired. Still, there seemed an awful lot of fans in the building for an event like this.

First up was the speed challenge. The Owls' top line of Travis, Sarah, and Dmitri against the top line of the Motors, which included both Cody "Hollywood" Kelly and Smitty. It was a relay race. They had to carry a puck around the rink, navigate some pylons, and then hand off the puck to the next skater.

"Dmitri's fastest," Sarah said. "He should anchor us. You go first, Trav, you're captain, and I'll go second."

Travis nodded. He knew it wasn't because he was captain that he would be going first. He was slowest of the three, and Sarah and Dmitri would know how much distance they'd have to make up if Travis was behind after the first loop. He didn't mind. Sarah was right.

Travis lined up with a kid the other Motors were all calling Wi-Fi, slamming their sticks to cheer him on. Was that his real nickname, Travis wondered, or one the producers had given him?

The cameras were all ready. They even had one attached to a wire above the ice that could be controlled by remote and stay with the skaters. The Joe was far brighter than Travis had seen it before. Then he realized the television lights were on – just like this was a real NHL game.

"We want you to change helmets," Inez told the six skaters. She had a helmet for each of them beside her, and an assistant was adjusting them. "Each one has a camera inside it so we can see what you're seeing."

"Great," said Sarah.

"You'll be filming my butt," sneered Smitty. "'Cause that's all you're gonna be seeing."

"Really?" said Sarah. "How charming."

Once they had the helmets on, Travis and Wi-Fi lined up and one of the assistants placed two pucks down on the ice.

Data had his thumbs ready on his smartphone, ready to tweet his play-by-play.

The producers had a horn connected to a huge stopwatch at the start and finish line, and

Inez joined in on the countdown to start: "*Five . . . four . . . three . . . two . . . one . . . go!*"

The horn blew and Travis dug in hard. Wi-Fi did, too. Almost instantly they came to the pylons and had to weave through them. Travis got through first and headed for the net, which he circled fast to come back up the ice. He hoped the microphones would pick up the sizzle of his skates – it had been perfect. But there was another sizzle to be heard: Wi-Fi was catching up.

More pylons in the neutral zone as they hit the halfway mark. Again, Travis was the better stickhandler, and he came through first, leaving only the final turn around the other net and a rush to the finish line, where he would hand off to Sarah.

"Travis digging in. So far Screech Owls still on top," typed Data.

At the blue line, Travis stumbled slightly and could just sense Wi-Fi blowing past him. The Motors had won the first part of the race.

The fans were cheering wildly. Cameramen were stationed at various spots in the stands, catching close-ups of the cheering.

Smitty took off with the puck Wi-Fi passed him, and Sarah was quick to grab the puck from Travis and take off in pursuit.

By the second set of pylons, Sarah had caught up to Smitty. As she roared passed him, she couldn't resist: "Where's your butt?" she shouted.

But Smitty was determined. He blew through the pylons, knocking one down, and by the second net, he was shoulder to shoulder with Sarah. Both handed off to the final skater at almost exactly the same time.

Dmitri exploded off the line, but Cody was no slouch and kept pace with him. When they came to the pylons, Cody moved through them like a slalom skier and into the lead. But that just powered Dmitri all the more. He crouched low and dug in so hard, Travis saw ice chips fly when he circled the second net. When he reached the blue line, Dmitri streaked through the air like a missile and crossed the line just as Cody lost control of the puck.

The Screech Owls were on top! Some of the fans began to boo.

Data's thumbs tapped furiously to record the Screech Owls' first victory against the Motors.

The three Owls line mates watched as "1–0" went up on the huge Joe Louis Arena scoreboard.

The producers had also arranged for instant replays to be shown on the scoreboard. Travis watched himself skating hard on the big screen, then saw the footage flip to another camera, a bobbing view through several pylons. "My helmet cam," he said. "Cool."

Next up was skating agility: Lars against – no surprise – Cody. The two competitors had to work their way through a complicated maze of pylons – no stick, no puck. The first through wasn't necessarily the winner. They would get points for speed and finesse, and would lose points for touching the pylons.

Lars was easily the Owls' top skater, but he was no match for Cody, who several times used his special move to carve as tight as possible to a pylon without touching it. The crowd went crazy each time he did it. Travis had to acknowledge, Cody was pretty good on skates, if not much of a puck carrier, and with his blond good looks, the cameras were loving him. No wonder they wanted to call him Hollywood.

The score was even. Screech Owls 1, Detroit Motors 1.

The competition moved on fairly quickly after this. The producers were running a slick show. Travis figured they were on a tight budget and wanted to move through the events fast to keep costs down. Or for the sake of the fans, they just wanted to cut out as much of the waiting and setting up as they could – the boring stuff.

Andy won the hardest shot, but Travis wasn't convinced the kid he was up against was the Motors' top shooter. Surely Smitty had a harder shot. When Travis had heard him ring a shot off the crossbar earlier, it had been louder than the bell at Lord Stanley Public School.

Data was thinking something similar. "Why aren't the Motors putting in their ringers?" he posted on Twitter. "Why aren't they playing to their skills?"

In the target shoot, Sam hit all four targets in ten shots, but Jesse had a bad time of it and hit none. The two Motors players hit three each. The

Owls were declared the winner, though Travis wasn't exactly sure about the math. If the two Owls had hit four targets in twenty shots and the Motors hit six, how come the Owls had won? He figured it was because only Sam was able to take out all the Styrofoam targets. Still, it seemed a bit cockeyed.

Screech Owls 3, Detroit Motors 1.

"We're happy to be on top," typed Data. "But why are we? How? Is there something going on with the scoreboard?"

This time, another tweeter answered back: "Why is a very good question . . . Getting warm."

Data clicked on the profile of the person who had posted the message – "VintageEngine" – but that was the only tweet he'd ever written. And there was no profile and no picture of whoever VintageEngine might be. The profile said he was male, but that was it.

The search and rescue event was the funniest. Fahd and one of the Motors players were blindfolded and, with their team calling out directions, had to skate to two stacking chairs placed at the far end of the ice. Fahd was to go first.

"Left!" the Owls shouted at Fahd as he began skating, stiff as a board, hands held out in front of him.

"Straight ahead!" they shouted.

"Right!" Sam and Sarah screamed together when Fahd drifted too close to the boards for comfort.

"Left!" Nish screamed.

"*Nooo!*" the girls shouted. "*Stay right!*"

Sam turned on Nish, her face blazing with anger. "You think it would be *funny* to smash him into the boards?"

"I was just joking," Nish said sheepishly.

"You've a sick sense of humor," she shot back at him.

"Thank you," Nish said, smiling.

Fahd listened well. The Owls won the victory when the Motors player had trouble telling her left from her right.

Screech Owls 4, Detroit Motors 1.

The goalie race was really no race at all. The four of them started out, in full equipment, and Jenny lost her footing on the first turn and went down. Sliding like an out-of-control car on an icy street, she took out poor Jeremy, who hadn't seen her coming. The two Owls couldn't recover in time to make much of a race out of it.

Screech Owls 4, Detroit Motors 2.

The crowd was on its feet and cheering for the final event of the opening round, the tractor pull. It was going to be Wayne "Money" Nishikawa against a big kid named Todd Carter. But no sooner had they announced the competition than Carter skated over to the announcer and said that he'd pulled a muscle in his leg. The producers quickly huddled and declared that Carter would have to be replaced by Cody Kelly.

Travis couldn't help but wonder just how serious the "injury" was. The producers seemed quite happy with the idea that Cody would be getting more face time in the competition. No matter, it was going to be "Money" versus "Hollywood" in the final event of the competition.

The on-ice organizers put Cody and Nish in harnesses and then attached each of them to a platform on what looked like short skis. Workers were standing by with skids of concrete blocks. They piled three on each platform. Roger, one of the cameramen, moved in to get some shots of Cody and Nish scowling at each other.

"We want to see your competitive sides, now, boys," Brian Evans, Inez's co-producer, shouted from the sidelines. His face was impossible to read, hidden behind sunglasses, a beard, and a baseball cap pulled down tight. Now he took off his hat and shook it for dramatic effect. "Ramp it up. Let's see some fight in you. Let's see some magic!"

Nish growled at Cody with his entire body. But the sound that came out of him was like an angry llama, and it made all of the Screech Owls laugh. Nish must think he's rivaling Cody for the limelight, Travis thought. If the producer wants to see a fight, he's going to get it.

Data couldn't help himself. He stopped typing and just posted photos. Angry-llama Nish looked ridiculous.

"When you're ready, gentlemen, *puuulll!*" the announcer said over the public-address system.

Travis thought Nish's head was going to burst.

His face was redder than the Red Wings logo in the ice. But Nish's platform was moving.

Cody was pulling fiercely, too, leaning almost horizontally and digging in hard. His platform moved as well.

"Two more blocks, please," the announcer called.

The workers placed two more of the large concrete blocks on each platform.

Cody and Nish dug in even harder. Travis could hear Nish groaning and sort of whimpering. Not a sound came from Cody.

"*Monnn-ey!*" someone in the crowd began to chant sarcastically.

Others picked it up.

"*Monnn-ey!*

"*Monnn-ey!*

"*Monnn-ey!*"

The chant rose in volume until everyone in the arena seemed to be singing Nish's new nickname with the most awful sense of ridicule.

"*Monnn-ey!*

"*Monnn-ey!*

"Monnn-ey!"

Cody struggled hard with his added load and could not seem to budge it. But somehow the taunting inspired Nish. Face red as an overripe tomato, he leaned, like Cody, almost level with the ground.

He grunted.

He squealed.

He whimpered.

And slowly, ever so slowly, the platform creaked – and began moving!

The Owls cheered, the crowd booed, and Nish, taking one tortured step after another, inched the enormous load from the center line to the blue line before falling flat on his red, sweating face. He was done.

Screech Owls 5, Detroit Motors 2.

The Owls raced over and piled onto Nish.

"Hey!" he shouted. *"Watch the hair!"*

But the Owls weren't to be denied. They pounded their hero and helped him out of the harness, and despite the boos and catcalls from the stands, they high-fived him and cuffed the back of his big hockey pants.

"Not a very nice crowd, is it?" Sarah said to Travis when things went quieter.

"No," Travis said, "not at all. And something's bothering me."

Sarah turned. "What?"

"How did they know Nish's new nickname?"

8

The producers wanted to take the Owls somewhere special. Brian – the ball-cap-wearing guy who kept stroking his beard as if it were a cat wrapped around his neck – was particularly annoying. He kept calling every place a "scene" and saying it was a "brilliant shoot," even though they hadn't gone there yet.

The Owls, outfitted head to toe in their magnificent new swag, walked along Jefferson Avenue until they came to Woodward Avenue. The *Goals &*

Dreams crew filmed them from a truck creeping alongside the team as they moved. There was no other traffic, meaning the street had either been closed off at the TV crew's request or else there was just so little traffic in the downtown core that it didn't matter if a huge vehicle was crawling at a snail's pace.

They passed a few empty storefronts and buildings with boarded-up windows. There was trash on the ground that seemed like it might have been there for some time. Papers were blowing around, catching in doorways. The area looked almost abandoned – a stark contrast to the flashiness of the events that morning.

At one point, the group passed a man with a scruffy beard, sitting at the entrance to an alley and wearing a ratty old winter hat with a pom-pom on top. Beside him, on a purple sleeping bag, was a small brown-and-beige dog that seemed content and well fed. But the man looked broken. He had a big gray blanket draped over his shoulders. An old margarine container, squished on one side, rested on the pavement in front of him beside a handwritten cardboard sign that read, "NO WORK.

ANYTHING HELPS. THANK-U." Inside the container were two nickels and a shiny dime.

As the Owls moved past him, they tried to avoid staring – they'd been told by Mr. D to keep their eyes to the front of the line. Once they were farther along, Muck dropped back, retraced his steps, and quietly placed a twenty-dollar bill in the man's container.

"Thank you, sir," the man said.

Muck nodded. "Take care of yourself," he said.

Several of the Owls – Sarah, Sam, Fahd, Lars, Jesse, Travis, and, of course, Nish – had been wired for sound, with small packs hooked onto their waist-bands and a wire running up the inside of their track tops and out at the neck, where a clip-on mike was discreetly attached to the collar of their new jackets.

Travis reminded himself to watch what he said. He wished he had control over whatever Nish said, too – but not even Nish seemed capable of that. What's worse, the producers seemed to be encouraging him.

Up ahead, Travis could see a huge bronze arm ending in a clenched fist. It seemed to hang in the air like it was in mid-punch. It was some kind of enormous sculpture, but it was so well done it almost looked real – like a giant's fist that might actually swing any second and knock someone out. Nish would probably take a picture exactly like that, Travis thought – of himself, in front of the fist, getting punched. Nish always liked to take cheesy photos of himself in front of monuments on their trips, and Fahd, who couldn't recognize cheesy if it bit him on the butt, was always pleased to oblige.

When the Owls arrived at the giant fist, by then all happily chatting away, they found a woman standing there, waiting for them. She seemed very official, very stiff. She wore eyeglasses with frames so thin it seemed there were no frames at all, the lenses floating in front of her eyes. Her hair looked like it, too, had been cast in bronze.

"Quiet, now, children!" she ordered in a voice that would bring a vice-principal to attention. They quieted at once. With an abrupt change of tone, she snapped a smile so fast it was like a camera shutter clicking open and closed. Travis almost started laughing. Nish did start laughing. He burst out with a quick giggle, then caught himself, and, red-faced, stood sheepishly listening.

"I am Marjorie Gibbons of the City of Detroit Historical Society," she said in a voice as clipped as her smile. "Welcome to the City of Detroit."

"Thank you," Sarah said.

"Where is it?" Nish said, another giggle bursting.

Marjorie Gibbons turned to look at him, her eyes burning so hard they seemed to weld Nish's big mouth shut. Travis had never seen anyone deal so effectively with his loudmouthed friend.

"Where is *what*, young man?"

Nish was rattled. "Just, you know, just like, well, your city seems to have . . . gone missing."

"Very funny, young man. I'll have you know, Detroit is my home, was my parents' home, my grandparents' home, and it is a city we in Detroit dearly love, in good times and in bad."

Nish turned so red he could have stopped traffic. If there had been any.

"Anyone know what this is?" Marjorie Gibbons asked the Owls, turning to the giant arm.

Fahd tried to answer – "A battering ram?" – but, as usual, was wrong.

"It's called The Fist," she continued as if she hadn't even heard Fahd. "It's in honor of Joe Louis. Anyone know who he was?"

A cameraman moved in closer on Nish, waiting for another of his silly one-liners. For reasons Travis couldn't understand, it seemed the producers had fallen in love with the Screech Owls' loud-mouthed, barrel-chested "Money" player. Maybe Nish really was destined for fame.

"Was he a hockey player?" guessed Fahd. "The rink's named after him."

Marjorie Gibbons shook her head so sharply it was a wonder her glasses didn't fly off.

Travis knew. He had the postcard of Joe Louis back in his luggage. But before he could speak, another voice piped up.

"The boxer," Wilson Kelly said. "World champion."

Marjorie Gibbons smiled. *Click.* Smile gone again.

"Joe Louis was the greatest heavyweight champion in history," she said. "He and his family moved to Detroit from Alabama when he was twelve years old – the same age, I am told, as all of you."

"Not Muck," Nish said. "Or Mr. D."

Marjorie Gibbons ignored him. She was catching on fast.

"He was the seventh of eight children born to parents who were themselves the children of slaves," she said. "Do you know about slavery?"

"*We play for Muck!*" Nish joked. He knew instantly what a dumb thing it was to say. His face looked about to burst.

"We know about it," said Wilson. "We studied the American Civil War in history this year."

Marjorie Gibbons nodded curtly. "Joe Louis's family was poor when they moved here, and they became even poorer when the Great Depression hit shortly after their arrival. It was a hard time. Joe Louis went to work to try to bring in some money. He even worked a short while on the Ford Motor Company assembly line.

"He was an amateur boxer, and a good one. He became city champ, state champ, and he turned professional so he could help support his parents. He fought seventy-two times. He won sixty-nine of those fights – fifty-seven of them by knockout. He was called the Champ, because he *was* the Champ."

"He was black," Wilson said with pride. "Like me."

"*You're black?*" Nish shouted, faking great surprise. Instantly he realized his mouth was again out of order. He turned even redder, if that was possible.

"Joe Louis was known as the Brown Bomber," said Marjorie Gibbons. "He is today regarded as one of the great African-Americans in history. He is hugely admired for rising out of poverty yet never forgetting his roots or his family values. All his life, Joe Louis helped others out. He used his money to fund inner-city projects that sent young people to school. Some young people don't get everything handed to them in life. And he had a personal code of conduct that is as important to remember today as it was in his day."

Data took a photograph of the sculpture, typed a line or two from Marjorie Gibbons's talk to go with it, and posted it online. Almost instantly his phone buzzed with a response: "A good person to look up to. Keep his code of conduct in mind and you'll get even warmer . . ." The tweeter with the mysterious handle VintageEngine had replied again.

Warmer? In search of what? Data wondered.

"Joe told those who idolized him to 'live and fight clean,'" Marjorie Gibbons continued. "He told people in sports, 'Never gloat in victory.'"

"You hear that, Nishikawa?" Muck's voice boomed from the back of the group.

Travis saw Nish's head trying to shrink, turtle-like, into his jacket collar. But it couldn't get down far enough to hide how red Nish's neck had turned. Roger's camera was catching it, too.

Marjorie Gibbons told them more about Joe Louis and Detroit while Nish tried to look casual in front of the cameras. The rest of the Owls lis-tened attentively. Muck loved anything to do with local history and the lessons that could be learned.

When she had finished, Marjorie Gibbons thanked them for their attention and time. The Owls began heading back to their hotel, the cameras still following them. Their visit to see The Fist must have been the producers' "Learning about Detroit" segment, Travis realized. The Owls hadn't seen any of the episodes since that first rough cut on the bus, so there was no telling what parts were making it onto the show.

Only one thing was certain: Nish's pudgy face, ridiculous bow tie, and dumb comments were going to make their way in there somewhere. No matter how well anyone on the Owls team played, the producers had already decided Nish "Money" Nishikawa was the star among them.

Back at the hotel lobby, the Owls who were wired were allowed to remove their microphones and they handed them to the camera crew.

They were waiting for the elevator when Sarah came over to Travis. She breathed out hard as if she had been holding her breath underwater.

"Phew! I feel I can finally talk."

"You didn't have much to say on the walk," Travis said. "Stage fright?"

Sarah shook her head. "No, not that at all. I just don't feel comfortable. I keep wondering what it is they're hoping we'll say and how they'll use it. That whole history-lesson bit – although it was interesting – it felt a bit too set up, didn't you think? Like the producers just sent us there to ooh and aah for the cameras. That's a good story – the boxer's story – but I felt as if they didn't expect us to iden-tify with Joe Louis, not really. I mean, the way that woman talked to us, it was like she didn't think any of us would have summer jobs until we're thirty years old. Like we're all rich kids or something."

"Yeah, I guess," said Travis. "We're not rich kids."

"Exactly. I dunno. There's just something weird about all this – something a little . . . fake."

"Oh, good! Sarah!" Inez flashed a quick smile as she walked out of the elevator and right into Sarah and Travis's private conversation. She gave Sarah a serious look. "I'm glad I found you. Brian forgot this . . . for the walk."

Inez pushed a small pink bag with a zipper into Sarah's hand. Sarah looked at the pencil-case-like object, confused.

"We'll get you all into hair and makeup before the dinner tonight at Green Dot Stables, of course.

But here's a little something for just walking around," she smiled, nodding like a mother hen.

Sarah opened the pink bag and peeked at its contents. This was exactly the kind of thing she'd just been talking about. Inside was a round cake of blush, a stick of mascara, a small, round case labeled "SMOKY EYE," and a shiny silver tube of lipstick. Sarah didn't wear makeup. None of the girls did.

"Um –" Sarah started, but she didn't get to finish.

"It's for walking around, like I said," chirped Inez as she marched away, her clipboard under her arm. "You never know where the cameras will be . . . or our dear Cody 'Hollywood.'"

Travis looked at Sarah, his eyes wide, but Sarah just froze.

9

As the menus went around the table at Green Dot Stables, Travis chose his order – a peanut butter and jelly slider, the first item his finger fell upon – without even looking. He wasn't *capable* of looking. His eyes were stuck on the glittery, blow-dried, face-powdered members of his hockey team who were sitting across the table from him.

The makeup, Inez had told them, was just for TV. It would make them look "normal" under the harsh lights the production crew had set up in the restaurant. But Travis was not convinced there was anything normal about any of this.

Sarah and Sam looked like movie stars, with sparkling tank tops, lipstick, pink cheeks, and hair that was puffed high enough to rival even Nish's carefully styled mop. And big Gordie Griffith, the poor guy, had even been given a fake tan to make up for what the producers called his "unflattering paleness." It would all look good on camera, Inez continued to reassure them, but in real life, Gordie just looked orange.

This is the reality of reality TV, Travis thought.

Green Dot Stables was a cozy restaurant on Lafayette Boulevard with a big, somewhat weird selection of sliders – that was why Inez and Brian had chosen it, they said. Most of the seating was in booths along the red brick walls of the restaurant. It was a funny building – Travis thought the brick walls made it look as though it had been turned inside out. There was even a little indoor roof. The producers had rented the whole restaurant: the Owls were all seated at one long table, and the Motors were at an identical table right beside them.

The two hockey teams – the only customers – had been plopped down in the middle of the room so the cameras had space to weave in, out, and around.

"We're setting up a special camera in the corner, and I want you all to take turns going over there," Inez said as she clutched her clipboard to her chest.

"Can't we just eat first? These kids are hungry," said Muck. He was standing next to a big photograph of a harness-racing jockey, and between Muck and the jockey, Muck was the more determined looking. Muck, of course, didn't have a single speck of powder on his face.

Travis could tell that the Screech Owls' coach was starting to regret agreeing to let the Owls get caught up in this production. *Goals & Dreams* wasn't the skills development camp that he'd envisioned. The promised "forward-thinking coaches" had never shown up. But that wasn't all that was upsetting Muck.

On the bus on the way to the restaurant, Inez hadn't sat down. Muck always told the Owls that standing was dangerous, especially when the bus was driving on icy roads, but Inez said it was the only way to get the Owls to listen to her. Nor did Muck like how her makeover crew had transformed the Screech Owls into hockey-playing peacocks. But worst of all, Inez had taken the one gap in their schedule – in which Muck had hoped to visit Hitsville U.S.A., the shrine to his beloved Motown music – and plugged it with what she'd called "character development" talks.

"There's not always time to eat, not while you're in production," was Inez's hurried response to Muck's question. She stood in front of Muck and faced the Owls. "But anyway," she added, "you'll only be away from the table one at a time. The rest of you can eat. And take your time when you talk to the special camera," she said, scanning the Owls' and Motors' tables. "You see it? It's just beyond that black curtain. That will be *your* time. It's like writing in a diary. You can tell that camera how you're feeling – how you feel about the other team – and about your hopes and dreams. Really be yourselves."

"I dream of having a mini burger named after me. The Nish Spin-o-Rama Slider!" Nish's voice boomed as he made his way back to the Owls' table. While the two teams had been busy ordering their small, round sliders – three or four apiece for some – Nish had gone over to the hair and makeup team to request a quick touch-up.

"*Monnn-ey! Monnn-ey!*" Nish started to chant, but no one but Fahd joined him.

"You're already on the menu," Sam chuckled with a crooked smile. "Didn't you see the slider called Mystery Meat?"

Inez kept going. "Roger will be roaming around, grabbing bits of conversation, bits of 'color.' We'd like you to be yourselves . . . to act natural."

"Oh, I'm a *natural*, all right!" Nish shouted above the murmurs that had erupted at both of the teams' tables.

"You *are*," Inez cooed.

"A natural pain in the butt!" Sarah and Sam shouted at the same time.

Nish sent them each a raspberry and took his seat beside Travis. Inez waved the cameras over and directed them to start filming right in Nish's face. The Screech Owls' loudest mouth, of course, loved it.

"The camera in the corner is for our 'hockey diaries,' right?" asked Fahd, who always liked to clarify.

"Yeah, sure," said Nish as if he dealt with such matters every day of his life. "We talk to the camera about ourselves. Like, I just have to say how great I play, and what I'll do when I reach the NHL, and then they'll put it on the show. Right?"

"Exactly, just keep talking," smiled Inez, only half-listening as she checked something off on her clipboard and started to type a message into her smartphone.

The Owls and Motors stuck mostly to their own tables as the sliders arrived and were passed around. Lars had ordered the fried bologna slider, Sarah the grilled cheese, and Nish had pigged out by ordering four: two catfish sliders, a Korean one (covered in peanut butter and kimchee), and one very mysterious looking "mystery meat" slider. Meanwhile, one by one, they went over to the camera in the corner and did as they were told.

Alex Dalle: "*I've been captain of the Motors for two years now. I wasn't even sure we were going to have a team this year – hardly any players had the money to come out. But everything seems okay. A bunch of players kind of came out of nowhere and joined the team around the same time we got approached to be in the TV show. But that was good. I mean, they're really good – some of them. It's kind of scary, actually. But that's how our team came together this year. Lucky, I guess. I'm just really glad we've been able to play. We almost didn't have enough players.*"

Sarah Cuthbertson: "*All of this hair spray and makeup isn't really me at all. I don't know what I'm really supposed to talk about here. Hockey? Then why am I all made up? Nish, the ignoramus, is more built for this flashy, fame-seeking kind of stuff. I just care about the game. I love the game. When I'm on my game, that's beauty to me. That's reality. The rest of this . . . well, this is just kind of fake, isn't it?*"

Cody "Hollywood" Kelly: "*I think we've got a great team this year. I'm new to the team, so are a lot of the* guys, but we're going to kick those Screech Owls' butts. You know, we're going to come out of nowhere. We're going to do it. We had trouble with the first comp, but this second one will be better. You just wait. By the time the actual game rolls around, the heroes – that's us, of course – are going to take over, like in every great American sports movie. Ha! I guess that's why they call me Hollywood. We're going to rise up and take over . . . it's coming."

Jerome "Smitty" Smith: "*I grew up in Detroit. This is my city. My mom was a musician – a backup singer, like her mom, who was part of the original Motown. My dad worked in the car industry. I love it here – but this city's in bad trouble. I joined the Motors this year because I heard there might be some bantam AAA scouts around, and that's where the junior teams draft their prospects from . . . I heard they might be checking out this show. I had to get in. I want to make a career of my hockey. My dad's out of work now, and my mom's not really working either. I want to make things better for them. I've gotta make it to the NHL. Can you imagine? Mom, Dad, here's a million bucks for you – bam! Go pay some bills! Buy yourselves a new home! I have to do it. That's why I'm so determined. That's why I don't play around."*

Wayne "Money" Nishikawa: *"I play defense for the Screech Owls. I'm the star player . . . I think I told you that. And stylish – the glasses, the look. Once I get my spin-o-rama move down perfectly – which I'll get tomorrow, for sure – no one will be able to keep me out of the NHL. I'm young, yeah, but once the scouts see that move on TV, they'll see that I'm a hockey genius. You have to scout geniuses early. That's how it works. Scoop them up before someone else does. I'm not full of myself like Sarah thinks – I just tell it like it is. That's what you're supposed to do on these reality shows, right?"*

"This is kind of weird, don't you think?" said Alex Dalle, the Motors' captain, laughing a little as she and Travis arrived at hair and makeup for their touch-ups at the same time. Inez had asked the players to make sure they got re-powdered – "to take the shine off your faces."

"So weird," giggled Travis. He sat down, and one of the makeup assistants began twirling a fluffy powdered brush on the tip of his nose.

Travis still hadn't introduced himself to the camera in the corner, but he'd gone over and hung out *beside* the camera, careful not to get caught in the background of anyone's clip.

Cody's diary entry had been intriguing, but not really surprising. Travis guessed that maybe the producers had made him say it. It just hadn't sounded real. *The Motors were going to come out of nowhere? They were the underdogs?* Sure, the Screech Owls had won the first skills competition – by a lot – but some of the Motors really knew how to play. If Hollywood was really behind his team, Travis thought, he should have been asking what the heck was happening out there on the ice.

But Hollywood's little speech wasn't the most interesting. Travis had been standing behind the curtain when Smitty made his diary entry. It was the first time Travis had really heard Smitty speak more than a one-word sentence. And the things he said! Even the producers couldn't have made that up. Underneath Smitty's gruff exterior . . . well, there was a good guy in there somewhere. That was the first thing that shocked Travis. The second was how deep Smitty's voice sounded.

"Your guy Smitty sure doesn't talk much," offered Travis, not quite sure how to make conversation with a player on a rival team while the cameras were roaming around.

"I think he's –" Alex started as the hair assistant teased the back of her hair into a subtle, sloping bump. "I think he's trying to hide his voice, honestly. I don't know him that well. He wasn't with us last year."

"Trying to hide it because it goes up and down like a yo-yo?" Travis giggled. His own voice hadn't started to change yet. Although, during Smitty's diary entry, Travis hadn't heard the player's deep voice skip a beat.

"Like I said, he wasn't on the team last year." Alex looked like she wanted to say more, but she just shrugged her shoulders slightly. "I think he tries to hide it because his voice has already changed."

Data and the Detroit Motors player they called Wi-Fi were also tagged out by Inez for some touch-ups.

"They don't like that I keep wearing the helmet cam – but it's mine; they just gave me the idea," Wi-Fi said as he reached Travis, Data, and Alex. "They say they want to do their own filming."

"But you're still keeping it, right?" Data smiled, motioning to the miniature camera now attached to the baseball cap that never seemed to leave Wi-Fi's head.

Wi-Fi nodded in agreement.

"What are you doing with the footage?" Data asked, fascinated.

"I worked it so I can stream online through my phone. Just a matter of hooking up to the wireless signal."

Data was impressed. "Nicely done," he said, nodding in enthusiastic agreement. "Really cool."

Wi-Fi smiled at Data. "Yeah, no sound – my mike isn't good enough – but still cool. And it gives me something to tweet about. We don't have fancy equipment to brag about like your team." He shrugged, still smiling.

Data just nodded. Travis could tell he was fighting back the urge to tell Wi-Fi about how the Motors' new equipment had been delayed but was on its way. He knew what Wi-Fi was getting at — Data had tweeted photos of the Owls in their new jackets. The producers had been pressuring the two teams to talk about the series online, saying it would create more viewers for the program. Data, who had taken the lead for the Owls' online presence, just as Wi-Fi had for the Motors, had posted the picture when he was low on ideas, and had instantly regretted it.

"I didn't really know what to write," confessed Data. "I just thought some of the new equipment was cool. We weren't supposed to talk to you guys about it, but I thought that online . . . it would be okay."

Over at the tables, Hollywood burst out laughing, and then Nish, not to be outdone, did the same. "Ha, ha, ha! Then maybe we'll have to *moon them* is all I'm saying," Nish boomed, talking through the french fries he was chewing. Travis didn't really want to know what the conversation was about. Nish took a big, sloppy bite of his Korean slider – one that left a shiny blob of peanut butter on his bow tie – and kept babbling.

"What do you mean, you weren't supposed to talk to us about it?" Alex said, standing up so Wi-Fi could sit down for his powder application. "You don't think we can take some chirping from a bunch of rich kids?"

"We're not rich," started Travis, realizing for the first time that Nish's new nickname could have more than one meaning.

Alex crossed her arms defiantly, but she looked curious, confused. Wi-Fi squinted. His shine-reducing powder was so caked on that he looked like a hockey player caught in a sandstorm.

"They just *gave* us all this stuff," whispered Travis. "They told us that your equipment, stuff like ours, had been lost. They said that's why you still had your mismatched socks and all that. They said we shouldn't say anything, 'cause you'd feel bad about it."

Wi-Fi and Alex looked at each other, wide-eyed, and then both turned back to Travis.

"They're the ones who gave us those mis-matched socks," said Alex, her glittery, mascaraed eyes now full of suspicion.

10

Travis had to admit it was pretty funny – even if it was also sick, violent, stupid, over the top, ridiculous, and . . . *wrong*.

Nish thought it was hilarious. He was laughing so hard beside Travis on the team bus it was a wonder he hadn't peed his pants.

Mr. D had been up to his old tricks. The team was heading out to nearby Dearborn and the Henry Ford estate for a session the producers had set up on an outdoor rink, and the Owls' manager had loaded a cartoon into the bus's video system that would last just about the whole length of the short trip.

Mr. D claimed the cartoon they were watching had been made twenty years before he'd even been born. It was called *Hockey Homicide*, and it starred Walt Disney's Goofy. It also starred Goofy, and Goofy, and Goofy – and, oh yes, Goofy. In fact, every single character was played by Goofy. He played Ice Box Bertino and Fearless Ferguson, the two stars of the Moose and the Pelicans. He played the referee, "Clean Game" Kinney, who Travis figured had to have the most wrongheaded nickname he'd ever heard of – maybe even worse than "Money" Nishikawa.

It was supposed to be a cartoon about hockey. All the Goofys wore skates and carried sticks, and there were pucks, but all they did for seven minutes or so was clobber each other over the head with their sticks and see stars when they were knocked silly.

Nish was howling with laughter, but it made Travis cringe. This wasn't hockey; this was someone's idea of hockey who had never played the game. Where was the beauty? Where was the fun? This was just head-bashing and laughing at people who got knocked out. Travis knew all about getting hit in the head. It had happened to him in Pittsburgh, and it had once almost ended Sidney Crosby's brilliant NHL career. Nothing funny in that, Travis thought.

Muck sometimes talked to the Owls about shots to the head. He said he began playing back when players didn't have to wear helmets, so most didn't. He told them his old teammate Paul Henderson had been laughed at for wearing a helmet, but today Paul Henderson is one of the most honored and loved hockey players in history. He told them they used to laugh off a hit to the head back then, and say a player had "had his bell rung." But now they know that concussions are no joke, and head shots have become hockey's ultimate no-no.

The cartoon got more and more ridiculous. Jet fighters dive-bombed over the rink. A whale burst up through the ice and dived back down again. And still players clobbered each other left and right until most of them had been knocked silly.

When it was over, Nish stood, clapping and cheering, and several of the others – Fahd, Andy, Wilson – stood as well. It was only a cartoon, thought Travis, but still; it was crazy what some people would do for entertainment. At least the producers of *Goals & Dreams* weren't asking them to throw in extra fights for ratings. So far, the Owls had only been asked to wear makeup and to sometimes redo a shot if the camera had missed it, but that was it.

Muck stood up, clicked off the television, and simply stared at Nish until he melted back into his seat, red-faced and quiet.

Muck sat back down without a word.

None necessary.

Travis had never seen anything like the Henry Ford estate. It was *huge* – larger than any farm he had ever visited. The house was like a castle, with heavy limestone walls – "Fifty-six rooms, including its own bowling alley," Data called out as he read from his ever-present smartphone – and it overlooked a river that had been dammed to power the estate's very own hydroelectric plant.

At the back of the large, snow-covered gardens, an outdoor rink had been erected, with real boards, lines in the ice, face-off circles, and two new regulation goal nets. Some of the boards around the sides had holes carved in them, covered in Plexiglas, so that the production crew could film the action as if they were right in the middle of it. There seemed to be cameras everywhere. For the next segment of *Goals & Dreams*, they had really pulled out all the stops.

Trailers were set up haphazardly in the parking lot – nothing like the perfect straight line of portables outside Tamarack Public School – and there was a lot of activity. A buffet food station had even been set up to feed all the camera and sound workers who would be filming the afternoon events.

The producers wanted the Owls to come into the largest trailer, which they called their war room. Inside were a couple of dozen chairs and, pasted up all over the walls, charts showing the story line of the episodes they had already shot and aired, and the episode that would be shot today.

"What's with all the Nish?" Sarah whispered in Travis's ear as they entered the room.

Travis had noticed, too. There were photos taped up everywhere as well, and it was surprising how many of them involved Money, the big, loud-mouthed defenseman of the Owls.

But Nish wasn't the only one featured. There was a photo of Sarah pasted right next to one of Hollywood, Cody Kelly. And there was even one shot of Travis putting on his jersey, his head just bumping out an impression as he was pulling it on.

Travis shuddered. They don't know I kiss the Screech Owls crest from the inside, do they?

"Okay, Screech Owls," a nasal voice commanded. Travis didn't need to look to know it was Inez. "Everybody take a seat, please. We want to go over a few matters before the actual competition."

Travis could tell by the way Muck sagged into his chair – as if he'd put on a hundred pounds since the competition at the Joe – that Inez had lost him. He'd okayed the trip because of promises the producers had made but never kept. He was losing interest fast.

As the Owls took their seats, production assistants handed out "scripts" to the players. Each had the player's name on it. Some were a single page, some several pages. Nish's looked like a small book.

"*I'm the star! I'm the star! I'm the star!*" Nish practically sang as he flipped through it.

Inez heard him. "You will be. We want you to improvise. Can you do that? Can you just sort of make it up as you go?"

"Why not?" Muck said dryly from the back of the trailer. "It's how he plays the game."

Inez sent Muck a clipped-off smile. Its meaning was clear: *I'll do the talking, thanks.*

Muck just shrugged and stepped out the door without a word. Travis knew from experience that Muck didn't always have to speak to get his meaning across. The Screech Owls' coach was clearly not impressed with the way this whole thing was going.

"What you have there are individual scripts," Inez said, smiling now that she had the Owls to herself. "They're not law, but sort of a guide for you in certain situations. We want to see you engaged with the Motors. We want you to have some back-and-forth, you know, take a few shots at each other, trash-talk the other side – what is it they call it in hockey?"

"Chirping," Nish shouted. "And I'm the master chirper."

"We're wiring you for sound, Money," Inez said. "And several of you will carry personal microphones. Those who aren't wired will also be heard, though, as we will have a couple of production assistants holding special mikes – parabolic microphones, they're called – in different spots around the rink to pick up every word you say. They'll be following the same action as the cameras. We want you to be yourselves, and we want some chirping – but please don't swear. We'd have to bleep it out if you do."

"I'd like to bleep Nish right off the face of the earth," Sam whispered. Sarah and Travis giggled. Nish turned around and gave her a raspberry.

"Okay, then," Inez said. "Have a quick study of the scripts we've prepared for you, and then we'll get you all over to the Screech Owls' dressing room at the side of the rink."

Travis didn't need to spend much time on his script. He was going to be involved in a couple of the events – none of them sounded particularly "hockey" to him – and he was encouraged to banter with Alex, the captain of the Motors, the girl he'd met over in the hair and makeup corner at the Green Dot the night before, the girl he'd noted was one of the Detroit team's strongest skaters.

He was just heading out of the war-room trailer when Sarah grabbed his sleeve and pulled him to the side.

"What's up?" he asked.

Sarah was blushing. She shook her script in Travis's face. "Have a look at this."

Travis had a quick read: "At the end of one of the events, Sarah is to skate over and engage with Hollywood. They've already struck up a friendship and viewer response has been exceptional. Money sees Sarah and Hollywood flirting and skates over to steal her back . . ."

Travis burst out laughing so quickly he almost choked. "What the –?"

"I'd rather die!" Sarah said.

"I thought you *liked* Cody," Travis teased.

Sarah shrugged. "So what if he's . . . nice. It's

the second part of it that makes me want to die! Nish is supposed to be my white knight? *Puh-leez!* You've got to save me from that, Trav."

"How?"

"I don't know. Just do something. I can't have them make a fool of me just for their stupid television show."

"Okay," Travis said. "I'll think of something."

But he had no idea what that might be.

11

Nish was out of control. Or rather, his mouth was out of control. The worst thing the producers could have done was encourage him. He was making an ass of himself.

During the warm-up, Nish scanned the Motors' lineup and discovered one of the Detroit defensemen, a big kid with an open, friendly face, was named Stuart Jennings.

"Hey, Stu!" Nish yelled across the center line

to the big defenseman. "Is it true that *Stu* is short for *Stuuu-pid*?"

Nish skated away giggling like a tickled baby. A cameraman ran alongside him, slipping and sliding in his work boots but capturing every word, every look, every moment of "Money" Nishikawa's chirping glory.

Travis couldn't help noticing that the more *Goals & Dreams* went along, the further it got from hockey. The skills events at the Joe had at least *felt* like hockey. What was being filmed on the outdoor rink looked more like a winter carnival.

In the Owls' trailer, while the crew had been setting up the cameras and the team was actually alone for a change, getting ready to play, Muck had made some effort to bring the players back to the game – to keep their focus on hockey rather than the bright lights and the "stage" on which they'd be skating.

"As many of you Owls have been told, Joe Louis was poor," Muck had said, and the Owls had all bowed their heads to listen. Then, only Data had been filming. "Joe Louis did very, very well, but he never forgot where he came from. He always tried to fight fair. It's said that he never, ever engaged in a fixed fight.

"Remember that when you're out on the rink. Remember where you came from. Hockey is like any sport: you're only as good as the player you're *trying* to be. If you fight fair, if you play hard, and honestly, you'll already have won something. The lights, the cameras . . . none of that really means anything."

It had been good to see the old inspired Muck again – even just for a few minutes. Travis was sure he had never heard Muck make such a long speech to the team. It had to be something he felt strongly about.

The Owls had then stood in a circle, banged gloves, elbowed each other, and tapped their sticks on the floor of the trailer. They were ready to compete.

But despite Muck's talk, Travis had to admit that the "stage" where they were competing was going to look great on television. The sun was bright and the setting magnificent. The air was so crisp and clean it felt like someone had freshly washed it.

The outdoor rink was gorgeous. It looked timeless, as if the Owls had stepped into a scene that existed a hundred years ago, fifty years ago, ten years ago, and right this minute – all at once.

This was going to be fun.

Brian, the producer who was deeply in love with his own beard, went over the first event with the players. "It's called Pig in the Middle," he told them.

"*Nish* in the Middle," Sam cracked. All the Owls laughed – and so did all the Motors. Nish's reputation had spread.

"The idea," Brian went on, reading from a piece of paper, "is to divide up on the ice into groups of four, with two Owls and two Motors in each group. You can use the circles in the ice for four of the groups, and two more groups can form in the center ice area. One player in each group is the checker. The checker has to stop the other three from passing to each other. Once the checker intercepts a puck, he or she becomes a passer, and the one who coughed up the puck becomes the checker. We'll pick one winning checker from each group."

They called out the names for each group. Travis found himself at the far left face-off circle with Sarah and the Motors' captain, Alex, who smiled at him, and Smitty, who didn't. They began passing while the cameras swirled about them. Sarah was first to check the others, and she deftly knocked a saucer pass from Smitty to Alex out of the air and gobbled it up with her feet. Smitty scowled. Now he was the checker, and the puck flew around the circle as he attempted to intercept. Travis was impressed at what a terrific passer Alex was.

Eventually, Smitty caught a pass from Travis by going down and extending his stick along the ice. He finally smiled – or perhaps it was more a sneer.

Travis was now the checker. It was harder than it looked. He would go toward one of the three, and just when he thought he had them covered, they would slip a pass to someone who was open. And the three passers kept circling around the face-off circle so that they were always finding new positions. Travis went down to block passes and failed. He tried poke-checking and failed. He went down on his stomach and stabbed, and failed. In the end, he clipped a puck out of the air and it was Alex's turn.

Alex stuck out her bottom lip in a hurt expression. Travis felt bad. . . . No, he felt *great*.

Soon the whistle blew and they all stopped. Men wearing tracksuits and skates tagged winners from the various Pig in the Middle groups. From Travis's group they chose Alex. He thought she deserved it.

Next up was the Longest Slide. Each player was to skate to the first blue line as fast as he or she could and then go down. The one who slid the farthest was the winner. Sarah and Dmitri, the Owls' two fastest skaters, made it all the way to the icing line before they stopped. Nish, the heaviest skater, made it to the far face-off circle. But Smitty, who dived straight to his stomach rather than falling first to his knees, was still moving fast when he knocked into the far boards. He was immediately declared the winner.

Soon after, Travis saw the Owls' coach walk away from his post leaning on the rink boards. Even from a distance, Travis could tell that Muck was shaking his head. This wasn't hockey. But it sure was fun.

Next was the Bouncing Puck competition. The organizers selected six players – three Owls, Fahd, Sam, Wilson, and three Motors, including the one called Wi-Fi – to dress in bizarre "puck" outfits. They looked like spacemen, but with huge inner tubes around their middles that were supposed to look like pucks. They were told to race once around the entire rink and were free to "bump" at will.

Travis had never seen anything quite so funny in his life. When the bouncing puck that was Fahd tried to bounce into one of the Motors, it looked like he'd just bounced off a trampoline. Poor Fahd went flying in the opposite direction and hit the ice, where he struggled like an upside-down turtle to get back on his skates.

Down the ice the other contestants went, the "pucks" bouncing off each other like pinballs. At the far net, they got into a traffic jam, and only

Wilson and one of the Motors got out of it without wiping out. It ended with a race to the finish. Wilson thought he'd try Smitty's trick and he dived as he approached the blue line, only his inner tube acted like a brake and stalled him a good six feet from the finish. The Motors' "puck" won easily.

Then they competed for the Ice Break Dancing crown. Loud rap music pumped through the speakers, echoing off the Ford mansion and the nearby trees, while all the players tried the wildest dance moves ever seen on a hockey rink.

Nish was center stage, surrounded by cameras. But so, too, was Smitty, who really could break-dance and was showing some amazingly athletic moves. The organizers went around the rink tapping various players, taking them out of the contest, until they had cleared the ice of all but two competitors, Nish and Smitty.

They cranked up the music even louder, the bass notes crashing off the Ford mansion like cannon fire. Nish was sweating like a pig, but he was dancing as if his life depended on it, even pulling off a pretty fair moonwalk on his skates.

Smitty, however, had his own moves. Down on his back and writhing to the music, he somehow executed an acrobatic "kip up" that shot him to his feet in one snakelike move, whereupon he began moving his legs in a way that made them look like they had turned to rubber, all the while keeping perfect time with the music.

The Motors – and many of the Owls – began cheering. The fans in the stands around the outdoor rink – fans who had seemed to come out of nowhere – went wild.

In the first skills competitions, Travis had been surprised at which Motors players the producers picked for some of the matchups. Now it seemed their choices were dead-on. The dance-off seemed to have been created for Smitty – he was that good.

An organizer went over and tapped Nish on the shoulder. It was like a storm had broken on Nish's face. Beet red, he cuffed away the organizer's hand and shouted, "*No fair! I was clearly the best!*"

Travis cringed and looked at Sarah, whose mouth twisted into a deep frown. They both noted how several cameras had moved in to capture the moment. Nish would come across as a poor loser.

A spoiled brat.

12

The final event was to be British Bulldog on Ice. Both teams were told to fill the nets with their sticks and come out to center ice, where the game would be explained.

Producer Brian came out again, slipping and almost falling as he made his way over. "This is a simple game," he said. "We select a 'bulldog,' and everyone else goes back to the goal line. When Terry here" – he pointed at a young man in a coach's outfit – "blows the whistle, all the skaters but the bulldog head for the opposite end. The bulldog's job is to tag you. The moment you are tagged, you become another bulldog for when the players skate back in the other direction. The game ends when there's only one untagged player still skating – and that's our winner."

Brian scanned the line of players, looking for a perfect bulldog to start. He stopped, no surprise, at Nish, pointed, and smiled. "You're our bulldog, Money!"

"More like *hot dog*!" one of the Motors players shouted.

Travis saw that a cameraman had been standing right beside the Motors player when he chirped at Nish. Brian the producer rubbed his hands together happily. The chirping instructions were working.

"Okay, players," Brian shouted, "off to the far boards and wait for Terry's whistle."

Travis and Sarah skated back together. "Sure didn't look like a random pick of the bulldog, did it?" Sarah said.

"They're trying to make Nish the star," Travis said.

"Or maybe the villain. Don't forget, TV is all about drama, and dramas need bad guys so the good guys will look good."

Travis hadn't thought of that. He had figured the producers were pumping Nish's tires because they liked him. It had never occurred to him that it might be because they liked what Nish represented: the perfect villain for Hollywood to defeat. Maybe that's what the crazy "script" had been all about.

The players all lined up, several of them chirping their opponents good-naturedly. Travis was looking forward to this game. He was one of the best Owls at eluding checks. He'd just pretend he had a puck and the bulldog was trying to check him.

The whistle blew. With screams and laughter, the Owls and Motors took off down the ice. But Nish had a trick up his sleeve. He took one look at all the advancing skaters and charged right at them, falling onto his back, stretching out, and spinning like the hands of a clock as he tried to take out as many as possible.

"*No fair!*" several of the Motors shouted. "*That's cheating!*"

But Nish just laughed and stuck his tongue out at his critics as he lifted himself off the ice to count the number of new bulldogs he had just created. He now had six dogs to help him out.

Data hurriedly tweeted his update: "Nish, the human windmill, takes out six players."

Sarah and Travis had escaped. In fact, Travis thought Nish had deliberately taken out as many of the Motors as he could. He wanted an Owl to win. So, too, did Travis. He had no idea of the count, but it seemed to him the Motors were having a pretty good afternoon.

The whistle blew again and now there were seven bulldogs to avoid, not just Nish. Travis got through all right, but Sarah didn't.

Travis huddled with Dmitri at the far end. "This could be over fast," Travis said.

Terry, the whistle blower, gave them a moment to catch their breath before the next run, and Travis skated to the boards, his hands on his knees, gulping air. While he gathered himself, he heard someone talking – not in a normal voice, but like an announcer speaking to a TV audience.

Travis straightened up and looked over the boards.

A camera crew had set up with the rink and the British Bulldog game as a backdrop, and an attractive woman reporter was doing a take while the cameras rolled.

"And so, here at the Henry Ford estate on this beautiful winter afternoon," she was saying, "the Detroit Motors have mounted a comeback to go down in history on *Goals & Dreams*. Up against the powerful Screech Owls peewee hockey team, and down 5–2 in Saturday's competition at the Joe, the plucky Motors have now pulled even in this remarkable competition featuring teams from two different countries – really, two different worlds . . ."

The whistle blew. It was time to charge back. Travis had no time to digest what he had heard.

The bulldogs now outnumbered the skaters. Travis slipped through, and he saw that Cody Kelly, with his amazing ability to turn on a dime, had made it, too. So had little Simon Milliken and two of the Motors. But that was it.

The whistle blew again. Travis didn't have time

to catch his breath this time. The five survivors dashed for center ice, but an entire wall of bulldogs was awaiting them. It seemed hopeless.

Travis looked back. He saw that Cody had slipped in right behind him, hoping to use him as a shield. Why not? Travis thought. Smart move.

Travis went straight at the area where Nish and multiple bulldogs were waiting. At the last moment, he deked right and dived, hoping to slide through the wall of taggers. It didn't work.

Cody went the other way, jumping right over one of the bulldogs who had tried to tackle him, and in an instant he was away. Cody Kelly was the last skater standing – the king of British Bulldog.

All the Motors raced to pile onto their hero.

Nish, sweating heavily and beet red, was muttering. "No fair *again*. If I hadn't been picked to be the first bulldog, that would be me!"

Sarah had been impressed by Cody's agility. She thought she should go down and congratulate him and skated in his direction. As she did so, she was suddenly aware that virtually every camera was on her, moving with her.

Cody smiled when he saw her coming.

"Nice skate," she said, and stuck out her hand to congratulate him.

"*Closer!*" Brian shouted from the boards.

Now Nish, who'd seen his beloved cameras racing away to film someone else, remembered his script instructions and decided he'd join in. He skated hard toward where all the other players were making room for Sarah and Cody.

Sarah saw him coming. Her eyes widened in shock.

Travis was between Sarah and Nish. He knew he had to act, and fast.

Moving quickly to block Nish, Travis reached up and slapped Cody affectionately on the helmet. "Good run!" he said. "You deserved the win." And then, grabbing Sarah's hand, Travis skated her away as though they were a couple in a movie, on an outdoor rink on Valentine's Day, knowing that his face was glowing brighter than the bright lights they'd set up for the TV reporter.

What had she said? *"Plucky Motors? Two different worlds?"*

What was going on?

13

"I'm gonna hurl!"

For once, Travis didn't doubt for a moment that this was exactly what his sometimes-best-friend, sometimes-worst-enemy, Nish, was going to do.

Travis and Sarah had to jump out of the way when Nish turned toward them, his face white as the toilet bowl he was racing for, and let out his familiar yell. Only this time, it was no joke. It was no silly grab for attention. It was real – Nish was going to throw up.

The producers were engineering more "scenes" for the show. For a "time with the team" shoot, they had brought the Screech Owls to Marvin's Marvelous Mechanical Museum out in nearby Farmington Hills.

"Great visuals," Brian had said, petting his stupid beard.

"Something different," Inez had smiled.

And nothing whatsoever to do with hockey.

Muck had decided not to come, preferring to sit in the hotel lounge, reading one of his thick history books. He had given up entirely on the idea that *Goals & Dreams* had anything to do with playing hockey. But he also felt he couldn't pull the plug on it. Not when the Screech Owls actually seemed to be enjoying themselves. He had made a commitment, and it wasn't right to bail out of something he'd committed to doing.

Muck sitting in a hotel lobby with a book in his lap was hardly a visual worth capturing for television, so the film crew was happy to let him be, and they boarded the bus taking the Owls to Marvin's.

And the producers had been right: Marvin's was incredible. When the bus let them off at a small mall and they saw the museum, Sarah and Travis couldn't believe their eyes.

The first thing they noticed was a giant clock – running backward. "If we stand here long enough," Sarah giggled, "it'll soon be yesterday."

They went inside and knew at once why the production company wanted to film this bizarre place. It was like a child's most insane dream. Carnival music so loud they could barely talk. Ceilings so high planes could – and *did* – fly under it, though they were all huge model planes, many with moving parts. There must have been fifty or more small aircraft hanging from the ceiling.

Everywhere they looked were pinball machines and music makers and strange mechanical creations from long, long, long before any of the Owls were born. There were even children's rides. One machine, when you put some coins in, popped out a Crankenstein monster, a ghoulish puppetlike terror that caused Sam and Sarah to shriek madly when he surprised them.

Nish had immediately sought out the scariest and grossest of all the attractions at Marvin's. Everywhere he stepped, a camera crew and soundman moved with him. He was being treated like a star and was happily acting like a star.

He came to one exhibit called *Dr. Binge and Purge*, which showed an animated old man sitting in a glass-fronted cabinet. Nish put money in, pushed a button, and instantly the strange figure in the cabinet began pumping bottle after bottle of liquid into his mouth.

And then, Dr. Binge and Purge began . . . vomiting. Back up came all the revolting liquid as if a horse had just kicked him in the gut.

The camera moved in tight to Nish's face as the blood drained out of it.

"I'm gonna hurl!"

Ten minutes later, Nish was back, his face returned to its normal flush, and he was again the ridiculous "money" player the producers so loved to follow. Whatever had happened in the washroom, Travis did not want any details. Nish was back to being Nish, and that was all that mattered.

The Owls played pinball machines and toured the museum. Travis liked best of all the mechanical bowler, a creation so lifelike it looked like a man carved out of wood was actually picking up the ball, aiming, and throwing strikes.

Sarah and Sam watched a re-creation of a group of sailors cutting up the last dodo bird. The sailors were little wooden puppets, and the dodo was wooden, too, but Sam started tearing up.

With the cameras busy following Money around, the other Screech Owls were able to talk freely.

"Have you asked Wi-Fi about him?" Travis asked Data, once he and Sarah and Data were alone. He was trying to keep his voice low so he didn't attract the attention of Roger the cameraman or Daniel the sound guy.

"No, I haven't had the chance," Data said. "I only talked to him at the Green Dot, and the tweets weren't nearly as . . . interesting then."

During the second competition, VintageEngine's tweets had become more and more puzzling. It was as though he were trying to send the Owls in a certain direction – his hints were all "warm" and "cold," like they were on a treasure hunt. But where was he sending them? And why?

When Data had tweeted about how much better the Motors were doing in the second round of competitions, VintageEngine had confirmed some of Travis's suspicions.

"Were the Motors worse before or did they just appear that way? Getting even warmer . . ." had been the mystery tweeter's reply.

And then, when Data had tweeted that he'd never seen a twelve-year-old player handle a stick like Smitty before, VintageEngine had returned with "So warm you're sweating!"

"Who *is* this guy, anyway?" Sarah asked, gulping down a giggle as Travis jumped. She'd forgotten to lower her voice. "Why don't we know more about him?" she whispered to Data.

Data shrugged. "I don't think he wants to be found. But he definitely knows something."

"That's why we should find out if Wi-Fi does, too," Travis whispered hurriedly. "He's tweeting for the Motors. Maybe VintageEngine has been communicating with him, too." His eyes darted around to make sure there wasn't a camera on him.

The Motors had been taken on a very chilly boat cruise on the Detroit River for their "time with the team" shoot. Unless the two teams were on the ice, Brian and Inez seemed determined to keep them apart. Even at the Green Dot Stables restaurant, Travis had felt that fraternizing with the enemy was discouraged.

Data began typing a private message to Wi-Fi, asking him if he'd heard anything from VintageEngine. But Travis cut him off.

"Just ask Wi-Fi and Alex to meet us somewhere in the hotel," Travis suggested. "VintageEngine . . . Detroit Motors . . . there's got to be a connection. We might need both of them to figure it out."

The cameras had been filming for nearly two hours at Marvin's Marvelous Mechanical Museum when Brian and Inez suddenly announced they had enough "footage" for the day and the bus would be leaving shortly to head back to the hotel.

Sam and Sarah wanted to have their fortunes told by the Brain – a bizarre, bald-headed, hook-nosed professor in a glass booth, with a huge, staring eye behind a monocle. The Brain looked insane. They were about to put their coins in when the Brain started taking verbal shots at them.

"*Why are you still standing here?*" he barked. "*I have other customers, you know!*"

Nish heard the Brain's strange, cackling voice and came hurrying over from the pinball machine he was playing. The camera moved with him.

"What's that wacko do?" he asked Sam.

"It's the Brain," Sam told him. "It's a fortune-telling machine."

"*Yes!*" Nish shouted. "I'm gonna ask him if I get MVP this tournament."

"We thought you already had that," Sam shot back.

A raspberry in her direction and Nish was digging in his pockets for a coin. He pushed his way in front and, with the camera right behind him, began feeding the cackling Brain.

For once careful to not be heard by the microphones, Nish whispered his question to the Brain. The Brain seemed to think about it a while and then shot out an answer on a piece of paper.

Nish grabbed it and began reading. The camera moved tighter, anxious to see Nish's fortune.

Nish quickly folded it and stuffed it into his pocket.

"What's it say?" Sarah asked.

"None of your business," Nish muttered, looking embarrassed. "It's my secret to figure out. The Brain is trying to tell *me* something – not you. You're not supposed to tell other people your fortune, anyhow."

Knowing Nish, Travis decided that "Money" probably had no idea what the fortune meant. Even if he wasn't superstitious, he wouldn't be able to admit that in front of the cameras.

"At least tell us what it's about – the topic," Sarah said, toying with Nish, letting him squirm a little in the spotlight. "Love? Money? Your future career?"

Nish, trying hard to regain his cool – to regain control – inhaled a deep breath and then let it out.

He's stalling, Travis thought, mentally rolling his eyes. He's searching that screwed-up brain of his for another awful one-liner.

Nish slipped his sunglasses down over his eyes and straightened his bow tie.

"You wouldn't get it, Sarah," he smiled. Then, to Roger's camera lens, he said, "Let's just say I'll *show* you on the ice tomorrow."

14

Alex had passed Travis a note over the roasted pork platter at the hotel buffet table. He read it twice, trying to figure out what it was all about: "Get off on the 63rd floor, turn left. Wait for us. 10 p.m."

He would have guessed it was a response to Data's message, but Sarah had already run into Wi-Fi in the front lobby: Wi-Fi said they had no idea who VintageEngine was and that, with all of the messaging he'd been doing with the other peewee teams cheering the Motors on, he hadn't even been following the guy's posts.

That night, after lights-out, Travis had tiptoed out of his room to meet Data and Sarah as planned. But Nish – who had been snoring like a hippo, clutching the little fortune-teller's slip of paper under his pillow like a winning lottery ticket – heard the door click open and got up to join them. He now sat beside Travis, Sarah, and Data, swinging his chubby legs back and forth on one of the hallway chairs on the sixty-third floor.

They waited. And waited.

Nothing.

Nish, who could never stand silence, burst out whining.

"It doesn't mean that at all, Trav," he moaned. He couldn't let go of a conversation he'd had with Travis in their room – one where he'd asked for Travis's opinion and Travis hadn't been able to tell him exactly what he wanted to hear.

Nish was convinced that the fortune the Brain had given him held the secret to pulling off his spin-o-rama move; Travis thought it might be a message about appreciating friends and family. Travis's sappy interpretation hadn't gone over well with his glory-seeking roommate.

Nish reached into his pocket for his little paper fortune and handed it to Data for a second opinion.

Data read it out loud. "In life, we are all attached by invisible strings. Pull your strings closer to you now."

"We are all *attached by invisible strings*," Travis tried again. "I don't really know what it means, but –"

"No, no, I get it," said Sarah, trying to stifle a giggle. "I'm sorry to tell you this, Nish, but it means you're not a real boy – you're, you know, like Pinocchio."

She moved her arms as though she were a puppet, and then flopped forward as if her strings had been dropped.

Even Data laughed.

"*Nooo!* That's not it either! It's about my *move*," Nish complained, trying not to laugh himself.

"Then I don't know, Nish," Travis offered, hoping his roommate would just drop it. "Fortunes are supposed to be confusing."

The doors to the staircase were suddenly flung open, and Wi-Fi, breathless, almost fell into the hallway, right at Data's feet.

"Your camera is all screwed up – it looks like it's going to fall off your hat," Nish said loudly as Alex, also breathless, came through the same door.

"Did you break it?" Alex asked, slightly panicked.

"No, it's fine," Wi-Fi said, insulted. He took his baseball cap off and began fiddling with the camera. Ignoring Nish, he said to Sarah, Travis, and Data, "I've captured something you're going to want to see."

Alex and Wi-Fi had planned to meet the Owls on the sixty-third floor because that was where the producers were editing the day's filming. The idea was to ask if they could see a rough cut of the show. And they thought they'd have a better chance if they had some representatives from both sides – especially Data. Wi-Fi and Data would pretend they needed a look to help them with their tweeting.

"But we were early," said Alex, finally catching her breath. "And when we arrived through the stairwell – you know, it's good training to do the stairs – we heard them talking. Inez and Brian were fighting. And then they said they were going up to the bar on the top floor for a drink – probably to fight some more."

"So?" Nish asked. He was still in his pajamas, with his sparkly Motown bow tie dangling loosely around his neck, and was half-asleep.

"So we ran," said Wi-Fi as he worked the tiny camera so it would stream through his phone's Internet connection. "Down to the sixty-first floor. To hide. They were walking to the elevators. Then, when they were gone, we ran back to meet you."

Travis couldn't understand why Wi-Fi and Alex were being so cloak-and-dagger about wanting to see this rough cut. It wasn't like it was going to give their team any strategic advantage, any extra knowledge about the Owls that they didn't already have.

"Why do you want to see this rough cut so badly?" he asked.

"It's not really for the rough cut," said Alex, grabbing Travis's arm. "It's for the raw footage that they didn't use. I'd explain, but they might not be up in that bar for very long. We've got a new plan – and we have to move!"

Wi-Fi and Alex's new plan involved a hairpin, a bank card, and a locked door. And to Travis's horror, it soon included Nish. Unlike the hotel room doors, the editing room (which was maybe a broom closet the rest of the time) opened with an actual key. Wi-Fi and Alex wanted in there, *fast*. And Nish, having gone through a brief magician phase where he had actually broken himself out of a homemade straitjacket (Sarah and Sam said he should have been breaking *into* one), said he was the one to do it.

Travis – who had helped Nish cut the locks on his "magic" straitjacket before his performance so they wouldn't have to be picked – was relieved when Nish jiggled the handle and found that the editing room had actually been left unlocked by the producers, who must have been distracted by their argument.

"One, two, three . . . and the money player does it again!" Nish bellowed, and the other five immediately tried to hush him. Nish's pudgy fist pushed open the door, and they were in.

"Maybe we shouldn't turn on the lights," Sarah ventured, clicking on the windup flashlight she'd bought for her Stupid Stop. Travis hadn't even realized she'd had it with her.

"Hurry, or else they're going to come back," Alex whispered nervously. "We can't let them catch us."

Wi-Fi hooked his camera up to one of the two monitors on the small but packed editing table. "First, we'll show you this."

The video started running. No sound.

On the screen, the Motors and Owls were at the warm-up before the second day of competition. Andy Higgins's butt moved past the camera as Wi-Fi, already on the ice, bent down to tighten his skate. The footage was obviously shot from his helmet cam. Sarah and Travis could be seen chatting briefly, then they both went after pucks. Nish glided by, using his stick as a witch's broom handle.

Muck, in the background, was shaking his head, calling the players over to the bench.

When the Motors, too, were called over to the bench, the footage went all wonky. Wi-Fi explained that he had removed his helmet and placed it on the boards in front of him so he could fiddle with the wires, but the camera was still running.

And that's when the film got interesting.

At an odd angle and from very far away, Inez could be seen standing with her back to the boards on the other side of the rink. She was barking into her cell phone. Then she hung up. Then she called back. Next, Brian appeared. They started arguing with each other. "No-no-no." "Yes-yes-yes."

"And watch this," said Wi-Fi as Hollywood, who was late for warm-up that day, walked out of the Motors' dressing room and straight into the argument.

"He argues with them for a minute and forty seconds," said Wi-Fi, glancing up at Alex for corroboration. "We want to know about what."

"I know this editing system," said Data. "Let me handle this."

The first file Data clicked on was the actual rough cut of the show: "*Here, on* Goals & Dreams, *it's a classic story of David versus Goliath, of those who have versus those who have not,*" said the voice-over as the footage cut from a dressing room shot of the Motors putting on their mismatched hockey gear to a shot of Nish rolling around on his bed, kissing his new helmet. Then Nish was chanting "*Monnn-ey! Monnn-ey!*" at the Green Dot Stables restaurant, once while on his way back from hair and makeup, and a second time with half a chewed-up Korean slider in his mouth and a smear of peanut butter on his bow tie.

"*They've had it all since the beginning . . .*" the voice-over continued over shots of Mr. D handing out five-dollar bills to the Owls at the Stupid Stop, of the Owls walking right past the homeless guy on their way to The Fist, and of the Owls, all dressed identically, standing in a circle on the ice, listening to their coach.

"*They have opportunity, money, self-assurance, and training. But having it all means nothing if you don't have soul, as they say in Motown. As every hockey player knows . . . that's the most important piece of equipment you can have."*

Then came shots of the Motors: Smitty telling the story about his family being out of work, Hollywood helping reorganize the pylons after Nish smashed through them on the ice. *"When you've got little to lose,"* the voice-over continued, *"winning can take everything you've got: blood, guts . . . and hope. The Motors began this week as underdogs. But for today's competition, the final game, they will emerge better, stronger, faster. They have no choice but to bet everything . . . if they want to leave this rink as champions."*

"What the heck *is* this?" asked Travis, his mouth wide. Sarah's face was empty of expression – she was so shocked.

"Did you see me? I was awesome!" Nish cheered, twisting himself back and forth on one of the cushy swivel chairs that had been squished into the small editing room. As the promo went on – they guessed it was a promo for the final game – they saw Nish stuffing his face at the buffet, and then going on and on about how great he played.

"Stop it. *Stop it!*" Sarah commanded Data, who slammed his thumb down hard on the space bar. "Now what *is* it that you guys are looking for?"

"We need to find an electronic marker," said Wi-Fi. "Something they might have labeled. Like Nish doing that stupid . . . I mean, that witch-riding-a-broomstick thing. Then we can forward through to the fight between Inez and Brian. If they left the parabolic mikes on, the ones that looked like satellite dishes and could grab sounds from far away, we might be able to get some audio."

Data pressed a few buttons on the computer. He searched the raw footage file for anything tagged "Nish" or "show-off." He scrolled through a dozen embarrassing options – from loudmouthed comments to on-ice antics – and then . . . *bam!* There it was: Nish on his imaginary broom.

Fast forward to few minutes later, and there was Inez talking to Brian: "I told you, we need the romance today. It has to start *now* or else we won't have time to make the story arc."

The production assistant holding the para-bolic mike must have been following the on-ice action, just like the pivoting cameraman beside him. The two were synched. Every time the camera passed over the area where Inez and Brian were standing – even though they were only in the background of the shot – the mike picked up a little more of their conversation.

Brian: "No, first we need to show more of the opposite-worlds thing – rich and poor, privileged and desperate. We can't say the Motors come from the wrong side of the tracks if we haven't established that yet."

Inez: "Establish it, but I want the girl now. It has to happen."

Sarah's cheeks turned crimson as she realized they were talking about her. This was how they'd come up with their flirt-with-Hollywood scenario. She'd been part of some cooked-up drama.

Then Cody Kelly stepped into the scene beside the boards.

"Just stop fighting," he said. Even though they were farther away from this camera than in Wi-Fi's footage, Sarah thought she could still see anger on Cody's face. "I'll do it, but Sarah's a nice girl. You can still do the underdog story without bringing her into it that much. You didn't tell me I was going to have to trick people – you said I was only going to play a hockey player on a winning team. I'll talk to her on the ice, but then that's it, mate."

Nish almost fell out of his chair. "What the –"

Sarah looked mortified. Tears were rolling down her cheeks. They'd been set up. They'd been made to look like spoiled brats to tell some stupid movie-style underdog story.

This wasn't reality TV; it was reality distortion.

Travis was afraid to look at Alex. The Motors' new outfits hadn't been lost; they'd never been bought. And the Motors had been selected for each competition based on their members' individual *flaws*, not on their skills. They were *expected* to lose those first competitions. The producers were only going to start playing to their strengths once they had the Owls on the ice for the final game. It was all just a story, written for television.

For a moment, no one could speak. All of them were in shock. Everyone but Nish had figured it out.

Nish was in shock for a different reason. He shook his head so hard, he did fall out of his chair this time: "Hollywood is Australian?"

15

"We're back at the Joe today for the final *Goals & Dreams* face-off. It's the Tamarack Screech Owls versus the Detroit Motors . . . ," mumbled a lanky sports reporter who was pacing back and forth in front of a camera, clutching his microphone, and practicing his lines.

"Okay, let's try it again, Raymond," his cameraman told him, trying to frame out the other reporters who were also filming live hits with their backs toward the rink. "I've got the Owls and the

Motors moving in the background now. We'll reframe when they're done their warm-up."

The bright TV lights were on again in the Joe as the Owls and Motors spilled out onto a freshly cleaned sheet of ice that shone like white glass. It was exactly the kind of pristine surface that Travis loved to take first crack at – only Travis wasn't there. Neither were Sarah, Alex, and Wi-Fi.

Something was off.

Brian and Inez weren't even watching as both teams began skating in circles in their respective zones, scooping up pucks and releasing them. The producers were standing, red-faced, beside Mr. D at the Owls' bench, arguing with Muck.

The Owls' coach raised his arms a few times as if to say, "What can I do?" But Inez kept debating. Muck shook his head. He put his hands in his pockets as if he was going to walk away, then threw his arms up again in exasperation – *or was he laughing?*

As Inez and Brian's faces grew redder and redder, Muck finally just turned away from them. He put his hands back in his pockets and cautiously maneuvered his big brown winter boots onto the ice.

Cody, Fahd, and Lars were the first to stop skating and stare. *What was Muck doing?*

Muck walked all the way to center ice – right to where Daniel, the sound guy, was setting up a microphone stand on a little red carpet for the show.

When their coach cleared his throat, swallowed nervously, and then pulled the microphone close to his mouth, every Owl on the ice froze. The mere idea of Muck wanting to give a real speech in public was beyond their imagining.

"Welcome to the Joe for today's game –" Muck started. The microphone screeched a blast of high-pitched feedback. He grimaced awkwardly toward his boots and then continued: "I'd like to ask the producers of this reality show, Inez Campano and Brian Evans, to join me here at center ice. A few of our players have something to say to you."

Both producers looked confused. *What was Muck up to?* They clearly didn't trust him – he'd been so standoffish and suspicious of them. *But now he wanted to thank them? Make a presentation?* With all of the cameras trained on them – with all of the fans watching – the producers didn't have much choice but to do as Muck asked.

Brian stepped through the gap in the boards in his running shoes. He shuffled slowly toward Muck, tilting his baseball cap forward to block out the bright lights, while Inez, inching along in high heels, clung to his side.

Muck looked mildly amused as they took their places next to him at the microphone. He waited for the crowd to go quiet. And then, with a quick nod to Roger, the main cameraman, who was standing beside Daniel at the control board, Muck abruptly stepped back from the mike and walked off the ice.

Above the producers' heads, the bright white TV lights shut off just as the four television screens on the electronic scoreboard flickered on.

Travis, Alex, Wi-Fi, and Sarah got there just in time.

They'd been up in the media room in the top section of the Joe, helping Data work his digital magic. Once they'd cued up Data's "special" edit of the show's promo – with the help of Roger and

Daniel – they'd raced downstairs, scrambled into their equipment, and burst out of the dressing room so they could be on the ice to watch the show unfold with their teammates.

"*It's a story of greed almost too real for reality TV*," ran the voice-over – Mr. D's best baritone imitation of the "Voice of God" the producers had used in their own edits.

Sarah started giggling immediately.

Shots from the last few days of competition played on all four screens: Jeremy and Jenny wiping out in the goalie race, Cody doing his fancy turns through the pylons, Alex stickhandling deftly through the course, Nish falling on his spin-o-rama attempt, Nish bowling over a half-dozen skaters in the British Bulldog game . . .

"*Two teams, from different cities and different countries, were brought together by their love of the game*," Mr. D's voice continued over the images. "*But the creators of this competition didn't share that love. For them, it was all about . . .*"

Cut to Nish chanting "*Monnn-ey! Monnn-ey!*" at Green Dot Stables restaurant – the shot of him yelling with half a chewed Korean slider in his mouth. Then, with full sound – Daniel had made sure of it – Wi-Fi's shot of Brian and Inez bickering by the side of the rink over how to "develop" their underdog story.

Underneath the scoreboard, Brian just stared at the screens as the images went by. Inez's eyes were darting everywhere as she teetered on her heels, fuming. No one in the audience moved. Like Brian, their eyes were trained on the screens above.

And there was more.

Next on the screen: a clip of Brian and Inez whisper-yelling at each other near the bathrooms at Green Dot Stables. Roger had recorded it secretly, but on purpose, while the players were busy lining up to do their video journals. "In case it ever came in handy," he'd said, smiling, as he'd handed it over to Data in the editing booth.

"If we hadn't gotten that kid Nish's audition tape and come up with this ridiculous show," Brian hissed in the video clip, "we wouldn't be in this insane amount of debt. Fancy buffets, new equipment, these production costs are killing us!"

"We kept that tape to get *out* of debt, remember?" Inez snapped back. "Brian, it was a *long-term plan*. Give it some time. We have built a great show. Nish is the perfect braggy, bratty show-off for a series about over-privileged rich kids. Our merchandise team has been *loving* the poor Detroit underdog idea. Now the sympathetic little Motors are going to win, and then we'll be rolling in money."

When the players had seen Roger at the breakfast buffet that morning, Sarah, her face still a little flushed, had been the one to confront him.

"How could you seem so nice?" she'd stammered while scooping a large spoonful of scrambled eggs onto her plate. "You were really just . . . using us . . . manipulating us." She was both embarrassed and angry. She was trembling.

Travis had seen Roger in the line ahead of them, but he hadn't expected Sarah to say anything. Not right away. Not until they had a plan. He'd half expected Roger to yell back at them, but instead the cameraman had leaned forward, smiled at them, and offered more of the story.

Inez and Brian, Roger said, had by accident received Nish's audition tape, which was meant for a different production office. They'd then built a show around it, and around manipulating young players into a drama they'd created, even though they were calling it a reality show. Roger and Daniel had been against the manipulation, but they'd both needed the work. Although now, Roger confided, they were both having second thoughts.

Travis felt the entire rink was holding its breath underneath the scoreboard screens as Brian and Inez's plan now became clear to everyone: pump up the spoiled-brat Owls at the beginning of the competition, then grind them into the ground at the end.

Some fans in the stands started to boo.

"Luckily, these young players don't care about your drama . . . they care about their game," Mr. D's voice-over continued.

The scoreboard cut to a final clip: Muck, giving the Owls a pep talk in the team's trailer at the Henry Ford estate – the footage Data had captured.

"If you fight fair, if you play hard, and honestly, you'll already have won something," Muck was saying.

Down on the ice, below the scoreboard, someone yelled, "*Yeah!*"

It was Nish, pumping his fist in the air to prove he'd been in on the plot the entire time. In reality, they'd edited the entire promo after Nish had gone back to sleep.

Cody was the first player to start rapping his stick on the ice. Then Lars, then Andy, then Alex, and soon every Motor and every Owl was banging away.

16

Travis wasn't sure what to do.

To kiss or not to kiss?

He was, unbelievably, about to pull a Detroit Motors jersey over his head. He had never in his life, in all his years in minor hockey, worn anything but a Screech Owls jersey. He had been secretly kissing the inside of his Owls jersey for as long as he could remember – his own very private good luck charm.

The other Owls all kidded him about how he had to hit the crossbar during the warm-up, but no one knew about the kissing ritual. It stood to reason, therefore, that no one would know if he *didn't* do it this time. Because this time he'd be kissing the inside of a jersey that, until a few moments ago, had belonged to the enemy.

Everything had happened so quickly it made Travis's head spin. Brian and Inez had been booed off the ice by the angry fans. Most of their production crew had left with them, but not Roger, the friendly cameraman who had helped expose Brian and Inez for the manipulative frauds they were. Daniel, the sound guy, was still there, too, now sitting in the stands behind the Owls' bench, wearing an old, worn Detroit Motors jersey in support.

It was Muck who made the suggestion that all the kids pile their sticks in the middle of the ice. The Motors all looked at Muck like he'd lost his mind, but not Travis, and not the rest of the Owls. They knew. They knew because they'd seen Muck do it before. Throw all the sticks in the middle, and Muck would randomly divide them up into two piles. Players knew which team they were on by finding their stick in one of the two piles.

Travis had ended up on the Motors side. With the fans on their feet applauding, Muck signaled to the Zamboni driver, who was standing by the glass, that he wanted a fresh flood.

It was Mr. D who came up with the next idea. When the Owls returned to their dressing room to wait for the Zamboni to finish, they found that Mr. D had set out all the Owls' original hockey equipment right in front of each player's stall.

"We were hoping you'd burn this one," Sam said, kicking the big bag with number 44 on the side – Nish's bag, the place where, as Sam once put it, "dead rats go to rot."

Nish shot her his usual raspberry and zipped open his beloved equipment bag, leaned over, and inhaled as if he were in a rose garden.

And it was Sarah who came up with the best idea of all.

"Let's share the new stuff," she had suggested.

Travis wished he'd thought of it. The expensive new Bauer equipment the producers had given them was the stuff of any peewee player's dreams, but the Owls' own equipment was all in good shape. Their regular socks and jerseys were in excellent condition. They all had nice skates, too, if not the shiny new Bauers all of them were wearing now.

"Let's do it," Travis agreed.

The Owls stripped off half of their new equipment and started to replace it with some of their old stuff. Mr. D and Muck carted the new sticks and pants and pads and skates down the hall to the Motors' dressing room. They also took half of the Owls' jerseys to lend to the Detroit players who had been drafted to the Screech Owls for this one final game.

Travis loved getting back into his old stuff. It *smelled* like him, not like new equipment from the sporting goods store. It *felt* right as he put on his old shin pads – right, left, right, left – and socks and pants.

The Screech Owls jersey spilled out of his equipment bag when he yanked out his shoulder pads. It fell on the floor and he quickly grabbed it up. He thought about how his grandfather always flew the flag at the cottage, and how his grandfather told Travis that a flag should never touch the ground. A Screech Owls jersey was obviously not a country's flag, but it was Travis's flag, and there was no way he would leave it on the ground like that.

But still, he couldn't put it on. His stick had ended up on the Detroit Motors side. He had been given a Motors jersey and it lay beside him. It was, coincidentally, labeled with his number, number 7, but with different colours.

It didn't matter, Travis thought to himself. He was playing for this team now. He was playing for all the kids who just wanted to play hockey and have fun and make new friends – not to be twisted and manipulated by a couple of devious television producers who were only interested in ratings. When Mr. D had come back looking for two more Owls jerseys to lend to the Motors players, Travis had surprised himself by volunteering his own.

He pulled the Detroit Motors jersey over his head.

And he secretly kissed the inside as he tugged it down.

The division of sticks had produced two great mixes of players. Travis and Sarah were now both Motors, so they could stay together on a line. But because Dmitri remained an Owl, Travis and Sarah were assigned a new right-winger by Mr. D, who took over the coaching for the Motors until a young assistant Motors' coach, the only one still in the arena – and apparently the only one not in on the lies – stepped up and offered to take on the role. Once the fake coaches of the Motors had figured out that Inez and Brian wouldn't be paying them, they'd all left.

The new winger on Travis and Sarah's line was Cody.

While the promo was playing on the score-board, Sarah had accidentally caught Cody's eye. The tall, blond Australian – it seemed Nish was right – had spread his hands apologetically. Sarah reasoned that Cody had also been manipulated by the producers, but all she'd been able to offer him was a tiny smile.

"Ditch the 'Hollywood' bit, okay?" Cody told Travis and Sarah, in his true Australian accent, as they tapped fists to welcome him to their line. "I already told you guys. It wasn't my idea. None of this was."

"But you're *Australian*," said Sarah with some bitterness. "You're not even from Detroit. That whole story about your parents and the mall . . . even your accent was made up."

Cody reached a glove forward as if he was going to touch Sarah's arm, but then thought better of it.

"I don't have any money – that part wasn't a lie," he offered. "When those producers found me, I was busking on a boardwalk in California – doing in-line skating tricks for money with my older brother. My mom and brother and I came here from Australia so I could try and work as an actor, but I wasn't getting any roles. We were going to have to go home."

Travis flashed Cody a small, sympathetic smile. He wasn't sure how he was supposed to react.

"The producers told me my footwork – from in-line skating and soccer – would bring something unique to the show – and that if this series took off, I'd be sure to get some acting offers in Hollywood.

"I'm sorry I lied to you. I feel terrible about it."

Travis could tell from the way Sarah swallowed that she was still a little hurt by the lies, but there was something in what Cody said that she appreciated, something mostly forgotten in this whole experience with reality TV: sincerity. The romance plot between them had been embarrassing and awkward, but Sarah clearly accepted what Cody was trying to tell them. He, too, had been tricked.

Besides, Sarah, Travis, and Cody were now all on the same team.

Travis looked around and giggled. It seemed so odd to see his lifelong hockey pals – Jesse, Fahd, Jeremy, Sarah, Wilson – all in Detroit Motors jerseys. Nish was still an Owl, but Alex had switched from the Motors to the Owls and was now Nish's defense partner. And there were a bunch of other new faces with the Owls, including Smitty.

Smitty was wearing Owls jersey number 7. Travis's jersey. With the *C*.

He better not have kissed it, Travis thought.

Muck had asked the on-ice officials to stay on – they'd known nothing about the scheming of Brian and Inez – and they were happy to stay and referee the game.

Travis felt his heart skip as the ref signaled both goalies and then prepared to drop the puck. He knew what Sarah would do – try and pluck the puck out of midair and send it across to Travis on the left wing. He was ready – and it worked.

Travis felt the puck on his stick. He curled back with it, his hands feeling more comfortable in his old gloves than they had in the expensive new ones, and he quickly passed off to Fahd, who was on right defense.

Fahd must have thought Dmitri was still out there – Travis and Sarah were, after all – and he tried the high hoist play that Dmitri loved. He lifted the puck as high as he could down the rink, where Dmitri would try and beat the defense and be instantly on a breakaway. But Cody didn't read the play at all and had curled back, too, thinking Travis might want to dish the puck off to him.

When they got to the bench, Sarah and Travis

explained the play. "Just head down ice like you're shot out of a gun," Sarah said.

"Got it," Cody said, nodding.

Nish was acting as if he'd been given his ridiculous "Hollywood" nickname back, now that Cody had dropped it. Nish was playing to the crowd, diving in front of shots, lugging the puck up the ice, blasting shots from the blue line, and pinching every chance he got. Travis swore that, at one point, he'd even seen the lights from Nish's bow tie flashing underneath his neck guard.

It was one bad pinch that led to the Motors' first goal. Cody had the puck along the boards and momentarily lost it in his feet. Nish lunged in from the blue line, sure he could take the puck away, but Cody, who had obviously played a lot of soccer back in Australia, deftly kicked the puck ahead so it passed Nish, clicked off the boards, and went right onto the tape of Sarah's stick.

Travis and Sarah were on a two-on-one break, with only Alex back. Alex was skating backward fast, but no peewee could skate faster backward than Sarah Cuthbertson in full flight.

Sarah roared down the ice, looking over her shoulder for Travis.

Travis knew exactly what to do: head for the slot and be ready for the back pass.

Sarah angled off to the side, drawing Alex with her, and once she had Alex away from center ice, she dropped a perfect pass for Travis, who was coming in fast.

Travis picked up the puck, faked with his shoulder, drew poor Jenny right out of the net, and tucked the puck in neatly as he soared past the net.

Detroit Motors 1, Screech Owls 0.

Travis was heading back to tap gloves with his new teammates when, suddenly, he felt his skates go out from under him.

He went down hard, crashing into the boards.

All he could see was Nish skating away. His best friend had dumped him.

"What was that all about?" Cody asked when Travis's line got to the bench.

"Nish doesn't like being made a fool of," Travis explained.

"He must be unhappy a lot, then," Cody said.

Travis and Sarah started giggling. They were really starting to like the player they were supposed to hate.

The Owls tied the game at 1–1 when Lars and Dmitri combined on a gorgeous give-and-go, Dmitri sending a backhand so hard and high into the Motors net that the water bottle popped right off the netting.

The players all made mistakes as they adjusted to new line mates, but Travis was impressed at how quickly the game took form, and by the second period, it had become a genuine contest. Players modified their games, some line changes were made by both Muck and the Motors' new coach, and it was astonishing how even the teams were, considering they'd been determined by Muck dividing up a pile of sticks at center ice.

Jesse scored a goal for the Motors when he tipped a Fahd shot home. Derek Dillinger canceled that out when he scored on a beautiful rush up the ice to split the Motors' defense and put a shot in through the goalie's five-hole.

The Owls got ahead 3–2 early in the third period when Smitty, who had played a strong, gritty game, took a shot, from the corner, that ticked off a defender's skate and slipped in the short side past the Motors' goaltender.

With time quickly running out late in the third period, Sarah once again won the face-off and ticked the puck over to Travis, who curled and passed back to Sam on defense.

Cody took off as if he'd been "shot out of a gun" – just as Sarah had told him to – and he flew past the Owls' defense, Nish and Alex, just as Sam's high hoist came slapping down on the ice near the opponents' blue line.

Cody was onside and on a breakaway!

He came in fast, his stickhandling a bit awkward – Sarah had told him not to stickhandle so fast, so hard, just let the puck ride softly on the blade – but it was effective. He faked a shot, then deked left and put a nice backhand into the back of the net.

Cody had tied the game in the dying seconds!

Detroit Motors 3, Screech Owls 3.

Travis was heading for Cody to congratulate him, but Sarah was there first – to *hug* him. It caught Travis slightly off guard. Sarah always hugged him or Dmitri when they scored, but this seemed . . . *different*. Cody, even through all the acting, seemed to genuinely *like* Sarah. And now, here was Sarah, laughing and hugging Cody for his gorgeous goal.

Travis looked back and saw Nish charging hard.

Nish's face was beet red, and he was scowling.

Travis remembered how Nish had dumped him after the first goal, and he wondered for a moment if he should jump in between them and cut Nish off from Cody.

Nish had his glove out, fist closed – just like the giant fist that hung out in front of the Joe Louis Arena. Travis thought he should lunge, but now it was too late. There was nothing between Nish and Cody, and Nish was coming in fast.

Cody had a look of wonder on his face. And then, at the very last second, Nish opened his glove and . . . high-fived Cody!

As Cody and Nish, now apparently friends, skated away, Travis noticed that a small, folded piece of paper had fallen out of Nish's glove and onto the ice. He skated over to pick it up. Guessing what it might be, he slowly unfolded it to take another look.

It was Nish's secret fortune, written in dark red ink.

Travis still had no idea what it meant – *could it really be about hockey?* – but knew that it was important to Nish and his ridiculous spin-o-rama dream. He quickly folded it back up and slipped it into his own glove for safekeeping before moving back into position.

There was another face-off at center ice. Then, a moment later, the horn blew.

As the players returned to their benches, Data banged on the glass a little farther down, calling Travis over. He was pressing his smartphone up against the protective glass.

Travis had to squint to read it.

VintageEngine had written to them again. "I'm proud of you" was all the message said.

"Ha! Great," Travis replied, smiling and gently rapping on the glass, ready to skate away.

But Data wasn't done.

He put his smartphone back up to the glass and then nodded in the direction of Daniel, the sound guy, who was still sitting behind the Owls' bench, still wearing the well-worn Detroit Motors jersey Travis had noticed earlier. Daniel was now standing, clapping for both teams.

Excited, Data pointed at his phone, at Daniel, and then back again.

VintageEngine, an old player for the Motors? Travis wondered. Could it be?

When the other players had finished filing back to their benches, Mr. D and the Motors' coach looked over at Muck. Mr. D raised his thumb to give the "okay" sign as the Motors' coach shouted over.

"Let's settle this with a shootout!"

17

"I told you, it doesn't mean that at all!"

Travis was talking, but Nish still wasn't listening. Travis shook his head and scanned the rink to see if any other players would back him up.

Nish had taken to the players' bench and loosened the laces on his skates, and now he was pulling them so tight it seemed his face would burst from the exertion.

Nish's fortune had read: "Pull your strings closer to you now." Travis knew how those sayings worked. They were a bit vague but always implied a deeper meaning. This one was about relying on friends and family, surely, like he'd said. And now that the Owls and the Motors had come together to take back their game, he thought he had his proof.

"In life, we are all attached by invisible strings . . . ," Travis tried again. "Maybe it's about how we're all in the same boat. All of the Owls are linked together. And now the Motors are, too. We won. We worked together, and we won. *That's* what your fortune was trying to tell you."

But Nish had decided it was a message that he should tie his skates tighter. "Says right there," he said, taking back the piece of paper from Travis. "'Pull your strings closer to you now.' I finally get it. *Strings* meaning *laces*. It *was* about hockey. See?"

Sometimes there was just no use arguing with Nish. He could be like a brick wall when it came to common sense. The brick wall was up, and Travis wasn't going to get through it.

Muck and Mr. D were organizing the shootout. All the players would shoot. Everyone would have a chance. If you scored, you were to kneel on one knee on the ice closest to your teammates. At the end of the shootout, the team with the most players kneeling would be declared the winner – though Muck made it clear they were all winners now. The team that had lost had a beard and wore high heels on the ice.

Mr. D made a lineup. Sarah and Travis would be shooting last for the Motors, which pleased Travis; he liked to be the one the team depended on, and he also liked the idea that he and Sarah would be counted on together.

Last on the Owls' side were Smitty and Nish. Nish was just coming out of the box, gingerly lifting one skate after the other as he felt how tight – maybe *too* tight – his laces now were.

The players were bunched together according to their teams. Travis and Sarah took up positions along the boards where they could watch the moves and see who had the best dekes among all the players.

"*Yak-u-shev, Owls!*" announced Mr. D, pointing in Dmitri's direction and swinging his arm to indicate Dmitri was to shoot first.

Dmitri roared in, faked backhand, faked forehand, then lifted a backhand high into the roof of the net, sending the water bottle flying. He skated back without so much as a fist pump and kneeled down on one knee to watch the others.

After that, they alternated, Motors then Owls. Jesse scored on a nice deke. Alex scored by going five-hole on Jeremy. Determined little Wi-Fi just went straight for the goal – his helmet cam running the whole time – and without even a deke slipped the puck in the corner of the net. Andy scored on a slap shot. Simon failed to score on Jenny, as did Fahd. And Cody, whose stickhandling might have been weak but whose skating was awesome, roared in just like Dmitri, imitating his perfect execution, only to lose the puck on the backhand.

One by one, the players skated down ice from center, took their shot, and then skated back to gather on the ice – the ones who had scored, kneeling. Travis only managed a rough count, but it seemed as if there was just about the same number of kneelers in Screech Owls jerseys as in Detroit Motors colors.

There were only four players left to shoot.

Travis's name was called by Mr. D, and he shot out from the boards, scooped up the puck, and raced down the ice, putting a lovely deke on the goaltender but sliding the puck just through the crease, where it slipped off his stick and was lost.

Disappointed, Travis skated back and took up his position along the boards. He sucked in his breath and looked over to see how they were doing on the other side.

Why was Nish skating toward him? he wondered. It was almost his turn. He should be getting his focus, planning his move.

Even behind the face shield, Travis could see that Nish was redder than usual. He could also see tiny white flashes of light behind Nish's neck guard. He was wearing the bow tie from the Stupid Stop. A good-luck charm?

"What's up?" Travis asked as Nish came closer.

Nish looked near tears.

"I can't feel my feet!"

"What?"

"I can't feel my feet – they've gone completely numb!"

Sarah started laughing. "You tied your skates too tight!" she said. "You're a real boy, after all! Look! Real tears!"

"You cut off the circulation. Your feet are going to fall off!" shouted Sam.

"*Nish-i-kawa, Owls!*" shouted Mr. D.

"What am I gonna do?" Nish whined.

"It's your shot, Big Boy," Sarah said. "Give 'em what you got!"

Nish seemed to be crying as he carefully turned his skates and began gliding toward the puck.

Sarah and Sam were still giggling, but Travis felt sorry for Nish. This was his moment of glory. This was the moment Nish had wanted, had waited for, had bragged about, and had promised would come: a shootout opportunity and a chance to perfect his spin-o-rama.

Slowly, Nish picked up the puck. It looked to Travis as if Nish was just learning to skate. He was taking almost baby steps, clearly in too much pain to move faster. Or maybe he couldn't feel his feet and couldn't tell them what to do.

Nish gathered some speed as he came across the

blue line. Jeremy, in goal for this shot, came out to challenge, expecting Nish to try to deke around him.

Nish made one deke to the right, but Jeremy didn't go for it. It seemed that Nish was going to go to the left side next and try to tuck the puck past Jeremy. But Jeremy read this perfectly and went with Nish, carefully protecting his net.

Then, suddenly, Nish spun!

He spun like a top, the puck holding on his stick, and Jeremy, now sliding with his pads stacked, simply slid right out of his own crease toward the boards.

The spin held, the puck held, and, in an instant, Nish had roofed a perfect backhander.

The spin-o-rama had worked!

"*Yes!*" screamed Sarah.

"*The spin-o-rama!*" Fahd shouted from the far boards.

Players from both teams hammered their sticks on the ice in salute to Nish, who was making baby-step strides back to the benches. Travis could see the tears streaming down his face. And they definitely weren't tears of joy.

Nish went down on both knees, then flat on his stomach. He let his stick go. Like a giant curling stone, he slid in to the feet of Travis and Sarah.

"My skates!" he whined. "Get 'em off! Get 'em off!"

"*Cuth-bert-son, Motors!*" shouted Mr. D.

Sarah gave Nish a quick whack on the butt with her stick and skated away. Nish was screaming in pain, and Travis bent down and began working feverishly to remove his skates. He didn't even see Sarah's shot. He didn't need to. By the loud rapping of sticks on the ice, he knew she had scored a beauty.

Travis had Nish's second skate off. Nish was still going the Bobby Orr route – no socks. His bare feet looked red and swollen on the ice. He was sobbing lightly now, but Travis knew his friend was feeling relieved. The circulation was coming back to his feet. He could feel them again. They weren't going to fall off.

"Did Wi-Fi get it on film?" Nish managed to stammer through his tears, his bow tie still flashing from below his neck guard.

"Maybe," Travis offered encouragingly, but he really had no idea.

"Smmmith, Owls!"

Travis had both of Nish's skates in his hands. He was looping the laces together when he looked up. Smitty roared out of the crowd of players, the last shooter of the game, and picked the puck up at center ice.

Travis was mesmerized. As Smitty approached the net, he used that trick only Sarah could do on the Owls. Smitty placed the back of his stick blade on the puck and plucked it up off the ice, turning the blade to hold the puck. He flipped the puck in the air, catching it on the front of his turned blade, and cradled it.

He was coming in on Jeremy, who had no idea what to make of Smitty's move.

Smitty then did – to perfection – Nish's spin-o-rama move. Only, he did it with a flourish. As Smitty began his move, he threw the puck in the air and spun in a circle like a top, and – amazingly – he batted the falling puck out of the air right over Jeremy's shoulder and into the net.

Travis had never seen anything like it. It was the greatest shootout goal ever. The players erupted in cheers and screams of delight.

They began pounding their sticks in appreciation.

"Get me my stick!" Nish whined.

Travis pushed Nish's stick toward him. What was Nish going to do? Throw it at Smitty?

But no, from flat on the ice, still crying, and with his feet bare, Nish joined in by pounding his stick.

Nish had seen greatness. And even if it wasn't in his bathroom mirror, he had to acknowledge it.

18

The shinny game and shootout had been the greatest fun the Owls and the Motors had together. The Owls voted to leave all of the new equipment – every single stick, skate, pad – with the Motors, the real Detroit players, like Alex and Wi-Fi, who hadn't just been hired for the show. Any equipment left over, the new Motors' coach said, would go to kids in Detroit who couldn't afford hockey equipment.

The Owls were glad to be returning to their

own equipment, glad to be going home. But they were sad to be leaving their new friends. They had new respect for Detroit, new hope for it since people like this lived here.

Smitty had come clean after his amazing display in the shootout. He was more than a year older than the peewee cutoff age. That explained his low-pitched voice. He said he had been approached by the producers, who'd asked him to be the "ringer" to lead the charge of the underdog Detroit Motors as they dramatically came back in the series.

Smitty was, in fact, a far better player than he had ever let on. That was why he did the amazing shootout move. He wanted them all to know what had happened. The producers had said he would not only be the star of the show, but he would be paid five hundred dollars – money he had already given to his mother – and they had also promised there would be scouts from the Canadian junior teams at the games. His hope was to play junior hockey in Canada, as so many promising young players from Michigan had, and then go on to play in the NHL. He had been lied to just like everyone else in this "reality" adventure.

They had said their good-byes. Sarah and Cody had exchanged email addresses and promised to stay in touch – whether Cody made it to Hollywood or had to move back to Australia. Alex had given Travis hers. He had blushed. So what? He liked her a lot. And Nish had even given his email to someone: to Wi-Fi, in the hopes that Wi-Fi might find some footage of Nish's spin-o-rama – anything the Owls' fame-obsessed defenseman could use for his next demo tape.

Travis was thinking about all of this as Mr. D pulled the Owls' bus out of the hotel loading area and down onto the street heading toward the tunnel to Windsor.

He decided to take one last long look at the city. He hoped the best for it. He looked for people in the streets and saw someone. It was the homeless man they had first seen on the walk to The Fist, the man Muck had gone back to and left some money with.

And he was wearing a brand-new baby-blue jacket with black leather sleeves.

With the Screech Owls' crest over the heart, and "COACH" on the arm.

**CHECK OUT THE OTHER BOOKS
IN THE SCREECH OWLS SERIES!**

THE BOSTON BREAKOUT

The Screech Owls are in historic Boston to play in the Paul Revere Hockey Tournament. For Travis and his teammates, the highlight of places to see is the New England Aquarium, home to seals and turtles and penguins. Its huge glass tanks are filled with an awesome collection of sharks, stingrays, and other sea creatures. Samantha Bennett, especially, is amazed, but when she meets an animal-rights campaigner who is keen to convert Sam to her cause, Sam falls under the strange woman's spell and becomes a new recruit in a very dangerous organization.

THE MYSTERY OF THE RUSSIAN RANSOM

The Screech Owls have never had such a wonderful surprise. A famous Russian billionaire has offered to fly the whole team to his country, all expenses paid! The billionaire, a big supporter of Russian hockey, wants the Owls to visit his homeland so young hockey players can learn from the Screech Owls' style of play.

But before the team's first practice on the ice rinks of Ufa, Sarah is snatched off the snowy streets and taken captive. Her kidnappers say they want ten million rubles in exchange for her safe release. Yet why are they measuring and weighing and studying her like a laboratory rat? Will the billionaire pay the ransom, or will Travis and his friends decide to take matters into their own hands?

PANIC IN PITTSBURGH

Travis's memory must be playing tricks on him! Did he really hear that someone is going to steal the Stanley Cup?

The Owls have been invited to Pittsburgh to compete in the biggest hockey tournament ever to be played on outdoor ice. The open-air tournament is to be held in the massive Heinz Field arena, home of football's mighty Pittsburgh Steelers. But almost as soon as the tournament begins, Travis suffers a serious concussion, just like the injury that sidelined Penguins' superstar Sidney Crosby. Travis is confined to his hotel room so his injured brain can recover. His memory is patchy, and he's having some weird dreams. So when he stumbles upon an outrageous plot to steal hockey's most coveted trophy, he can't be sure if his mind is playing tricks or whether the danger is a terrible reality.

FACE-OFF
AT THE ALAMO

The Screech Owls are deep in the heart of Texas, in the
southern city of San Antonio. The town is a surprising
hotbed of American ice hockey, and the Owls are excited to
come and play in the big San Antonio Peewee Invitational.
Between games, they can explore the fascinating canals that
twist and turn through the city's historic downtown.

The tournament has been set up to include guided
tours of the Alamo, the world's most famous fort, where
Davy Crockett fought and died. The championship-winning
team will even get to spend a night in the historic fort.

The Screech Owls discover that the Alamo is America's
greatest symbol of courage and freedom, and when Travis and
his friends uncover a secret plot to destroy it, they must
summon all the courage of the fort's original defenders.

MYSTERY AT LAKE PLACID

Travis Lindsay, his best friend, Nish, and all their pals on the Screech Owls hockey team are on their way to New York for an international peewee tournament. As the team makes its way to Lake Placid, excitement builds with the prospect of playing on an Olympic rink, in a huge arena, scouts in the stands!

But as soon as they arrive, things start to go wrong. Their star center, Sarah, plays badly. Travis gets knocked down in the street. And someone starts tampering with the equipment. Who is trying to sabotage the Screech Owls? And can Travis and the others stop the destruction before the final game?

THE NIGHT THEY STOLE THE STANLEY CUP

Someone is out to steal the Stanley Cup – and only the Screech Owls stand between the thieves and their prize!

Travis, Nish, and the rest of the Screech Owls have come to Toronto for the biggest hockey tournament of their lives – only to find themselves in the biggest *mess* of their lives. First, Nish sprains his ankle falling down the stairs at the CN Tower. Later, key members of the team get caught shoplifting. And during a tour of the Hockey Hall of Fame, Travis overhears two men plotting to snatch the priceless Stanley Cup and hold it for ransom!

Can the Screech Owls do anything to save the most revered trophy in the country? And can they rise to the challenge on the ice and play their best hockey ever?

THE GHOST OF THE STANLEY CUP

The Screech Owls have come to Ottawa to play in the Little Stanley Cup Peewee Tournament. This relaxed summer event honors Lord Stanley himself – the man who donated the Stanley Cup to hockey – and gives young players a chance to see the wonders of Canada's capital city, travel into the wilds of Algonquin Park, and even go river rafting.

Their manager, Mr. Dillinger, is also taking them to visit some of the region's famous ghosts: the ghost of a dead prime minister, the ghost of a man hanged for murder, the ghost of the famous painter Tom Thomson. At first the Owls think this is Mr. Dillinger's best idea ever, until Travis and his friends begin to suspect that one of these ghosts could be real.

Who is this phantom? Why has he come to haunt the Screech Owls? And what is his connection to the mysterious young stranger who offers to coach the team?

SUDDEN DEATH IN NEW YORK CITY

Nish has done some crazy things – but nothing to match this! At midnight on New Year's Eve, he plans to "moon" the entire world.

The Screech Owls are in New York City for the Big Apple International Peewee Tournament. Not only will they play hockey in Madison Square Garden, home of the New York Rangers, but on New Year's Eve they'll be going to Times Square for the live broadcast of the countdown to midnight. It will be shown on a giant TV screen and beamed around the world by a satellite. Data and Fahd soon discover that, with just a laptop and video camera, they can interrupt the broadcast – and Nish will be able to pull off the most outrageous stunt ever.

Just hours before midnight, the Screech Owls learn that terrorists plan to disrupt the New Year's celebration. What will Nish do now? And what will happen at the biggest party in history?

PERIL AT THE WORLD'S BIGGEST HOCKEY TOURNAMENT

The Screech Owls have convinced their coach, Muck, to let them play in the Bell Capital Cup in Ottawa, even though it means spending New Year's away from their families. It's a chance to skate on the same ice rink where Wayne Gretzky played his last game in Canada, and where NHLers like Daniel Alfredsson, Sidney Crosby, and Mario Lemieux have played.

During the tournament, political leaders from around the world are meeting in Ottawa. To pay tribute to the young hockey players, the prime minister has invited the leaders to watch the final game on New Year's Day. The Owls can barely contain their excitement!

Meanwhile, as Nish is nursing an injured knee off-ice, he may have finally found a way to get into the *Guinness World Records*. But what no one knows is that a diabolical terrorist also has plans to make it a memorable – and deadly – game.

SCREECH OWLS

ROY MacGREGOR was named a media inductee to the Hockey Hall of Fame in 2012, when he was given the Elmer Ferguson Memorial Award for excellence in hockey journalism. He has been involved in hockey all his life, from playing all-star hockey in Huntsville, Ontario, against the likes of Bobby Orr from nearby Parry Sound, to coaching, and he is still playing old-timers hockey in Ottawa, where he lives with his wife, Ellen. They have four grown children. He was inspired to write *The Highest Number in the World*, illustrated by Geneviève Després, when his now grown-up daughter started playing hockey as a young girl. Roy is also the author of several classics in hockey literature. *The Home Team: Fathers, Sons and Hockey* was shortlisted for the Governor General's Award for Literature. *Home Game: Hockey and Life in Canada* (written with Ken Dryden) was a bestseller, as were *Road Games: A Year in the Life of the NHL*, *The Seven A.M. Practice*, and his latest, *Wayne Gretzky's Ghost: And Other Tales from a Lifetime in Hockey*. He wrote *Mystery at Lake Placid*, the first book in the bestselling, internationally successful Screech Owls series in 1995. In 2005, Roy was named an Officer of the Order of Canada.